THE ZUYTDORP SURVIVORS

THE ZUYTDORP SURVIVORS

Nigel Clayton

First published in Australia by
Meni Publishing and Binding in 2008
Copyright © Nigel Clayton, 2008
This edition: Zuytdorp Press, 2022

The National Library of Australia Cataloguing-in-Publication
'original' data:

The Zuytdorp Survivors, 1st ed.
ISBN 978 0 6454632 7 9
1. Zuytdorp (ship) – Fiction. 2. Shipwreck victims – Western
Australia - Fiction. I. Title.
A823.4

BISAC
FIC014000   FICTION / Historical / General
FIC002000   FICTION / Action & Adventure
FIC000000   FICTION / General

Poetry/story book - Children

A Pygmy Possum Named Henry
A Turtle Named Myrtle
A Crow Named Wahn
A Girl Named Castor

Adult poetry by this author:

Afghan - Song of the Desert
Orcinus Orca - Song of the Ocean
Hollandia Nova - Song of the Coast
Kibeho - An Epic Poem
Song of the Templar
Songs of Australia - A Poetic Trilogy
1453 - Constantinople

Other Titles

The Long Road to Rwanda
The Templar: and the City of God [Part 1]
The Templar: and the Temple of Káros [Part 2]
The Templar: and the Cross of Christ [Part 3]
Amazon [Part 4 of The Templar series]
Chivalry [Omnibus]
Underworld
Templar, Assassination, Trial & Torture
Dreamtime - An Aboriginal Odyssey
This Pestilence, Bergen-Belsen
When the Virgin Falls
Colonies of Earth [Also known as Mildratawa]
Fall of the Inca Empire
The Kibeho Massacre: As It Happened
Afghan Camel Strings and the Australian Outback
Tom of Twofold Bay
Afghan - The Script
Kibeho - Original Script

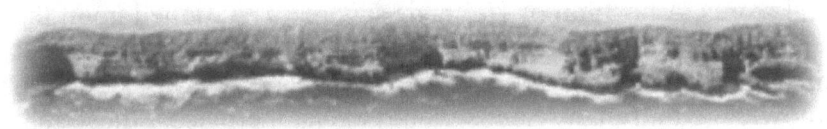

HISTORY

The Dutch United East India Company (Vereenigde Oost-Indische Compagnie – VOC) was the most powerful company at the time of the Zuytdorp, and the Zuytdorp was one of their largest ships. A great monopoly stretched from Holland to Asia – namely Batavia (Jakarta) where the VOC headquarters was established – and other countries, which were a source of great wealth and commodity. Within time the VOC boasted settlements in Java, Sumatra, Borneo, India, Ceylon, Arabia, Persia, Bengal, Malacca, Celebs, Timor, China and Japan. Trade between these centres was also of strategic importance where trade and wealth was concerned, copper, tin, spices, opium and dyes being basic requisites of commerce.

Spices were something that was new to Europe, tantalizing fragments, granules and flakes, or powered, that inspired great satisfaction within all across the country, each and every one tired of the tasteless morsels dished out at dinner time and turning to spices en masse.

In more cases than not the ideal time for departing on these grand ventures across the seas, where it was usual for more than one ship to be in the company on another, was in December or April, eight months forecast for the voyage ahead, and this after being provided the mandatory and rather necessary rest stop at the Cape of Good Hope, Table Bay, for a period of ten days, a period of time which had been cut drastically from an extravagant three to four weeks. There was a fort here, established in 1652 for the sole purpose of providing medical aid and stores. A hospital of 200 beds saw many stationed upon the seafaring ships take harbour within the facility to fight that dreaded scourge of the seas, scurvy, and it was common knowledge that many hands would exchange places, those that had commenced a journey from Holland not necessarily completing the trip with that posting; it was another sad fact that all had to face and that was the death rate for those on such a long voyage, for quite a large portion of the ship's company would come to grief and be launched into the sea covered in sacking; savoury morsels for the fishes.

To avoid the dangers of the coast, from Table Bay to Batavia, at a time when the Portuguese were an enemy to be avoided, an alternate route was discovered: which also alleviated the problems in regards to wind direction. The ships would travel due west for approximately 1,000 Dutch miles before turning north. It was unfortunate, however, that there was no means by which to accurately determine longitude at sea, latitude on the other hand was quite reliable. Eventually land was encountered and this then became the accepted method of voyage: to seek the sight of land and then head north towards the coast of Sumatra. For almost a hundred years some were lucky enough to cast their eyes upon the west coast of a great mass of land, thought to have been part of New Guinea. Many names were cast upon the landmass, eventually Nova Hollandia taking hold: or as the age-wearied maps prove, Hollandia Nova. Only one real warning of impending danger was forecast to the captains of these ships and that was to avoid the Triall Rocks [the spelling is misconstrued for Trial comes from Tryall, sometimes spelled as Tryal, so Triall could essentially be correct, as seen recorded on numerous occasions] as the submerged capacity of the hidden encumbrance was enough to see a ship easily bashed, sliced, and quartered.

The Zuytdorp was considered by many as the largest ship

within the VOC and only two others were of equal size. It was built between 23 Dec 1700 and 22 June 1701, being 160 feet long, 40 feet wide, and the depth of the hold was 17 feet (283 millimetres to the Amsterdam foot). She was capable of carrying 250 lasts (500 tons) which towards the latter portion of her life was increased on paper and task: the Zuytdorp in 1712 carried in the vicinity of 576 lasts.

The Zuytdorp, due to the situation with war and pirates, carried ten 12-pound guns, twenty-two 8-pound guns and eight 4-pound guns (swivel cannons). The swivel and two 8-pounders were made of bronze; all others were iron muzzle loaders.

The Zuytdorp and Belvliet had set sail for the Cape of Good Hope, to journey for most of the voyage within sight of one another, but there were instances where they were to become separated, for one reason or another. The voyage was treacherous to say the least; a longer than expected journey being suffered as the ships had to sail up and around Scotland in order to avoid English ships of the sea patrolling the Channel.

The Zuytdorp arrived at the Cape of Good Hope on 23rd March 1712, and of the original 286 crew had lost 112 men and had 22 sick on board; eight having deserted at São Tomé; most deaths are attributed to scurvy but others of tropical malaria from São Tomé itself. The Belvliet fared little better, percentage wise, and arrived on 27th March, and from a crew of 164 had lost 60 dead and 18 sick, with two desertions at São Tomé.

Much time was then spent at the Cape to replenish men and stores when finally, on 22 April 1712, the Zuytdorp departed the Cape with the ship Kockenge; the Belvliet departing several weeks later on the 9th May.

The Zuytdorp pulled ahead of the Kockenge due to her being a much larger and faster vessel, a vessel of the first class, 200 'eaters' (people) on board, 80-90 of them being new to the ship. Due to the departure being in April, opposed to the favourable

March, the captain decided to sail until sighting land before turning north for Sunda Strait, to take good advantage of the winds from the west and the voyage then to the north.

But catastrophe is all they meet, no success in voyage to be celebrated. This is their story, the story of the survivors of the Zuytdorp, a part of history that is known by few, and those few are none other than the survivors, and their legacy.

GENERAL NOTE

There was no single, homogeneous Aboriginal society, but around 250 different tribes and well in excess of 100 different dialects spoken, the difference between the languages in some cases were as comparable to English and Portuguese. With such a vast network of tribal backgrounds and varying ceremonial beliefs, where interaction between groups was a common occurrence, it is not surprising to understand how members of a tribe were multilingual and able to quite effectively speak 10 different dialects or more.

The differences between tribes were as different as chalk and cheese: their language was different; their customs, kinship systems, ceremonial music and dance... all had its place, but some were used as tools of trade.

Where subtle interaction was sought between the different clans in order to pursue marriage, partners for boys coming of adulthood and of girls ready to enter into sacred ceremony, groups were bonded by belief and enactment. New myths could hence be strung, beliefs exchanged, strategies of the hunt and food gathering techniques discussed. A cycle of life and survival was maintained and the gene pool stirred well to prevent the curse-of-ancestors from rising from the dead.

There is also one other aspect of aboriginal life which must be made quite clear, and it certainly isn't considered normal, but quite the opposite, and that is in respect to the genes. There is evidence [in the 20th Century] to show that Aboriginals of the Shark Bay area suffer from Porphyria Variegate, a gene mutation that is traceable to the Dutch, as is the disease in South Africa where 1 in 300 persons suffer from it. It is uncommon and rare, and there is no reason, other than the coupling of an Aboriginal with a survivor of the Zuytdorp, that currently explains the disease being discovered in Australia.

But for the most part there was peace amongst the Aboriginals, right across the land.

In 1623, Jan Carstenz put colourful descriptions to several armed encounters with the Aboriginals. He spoke of how arid the land was, of how inhospitable and barren the entire place was, where no such horrid place existed anywhere else on earth. He spoke of the inhabitants as the most wretched and poorest that he had ever seen. These comments were carried quite literally back to the Netherlands, and the Dutch government decided that the land was not suitable for colonisation and no benefit could be won from seeking such an endeavour.

It is not surprising therefore that all the men and women that saw the land from far out to sea felt the fear build up within them, a fear suddenly drowned by the so deeply satisfying and secure feeling within, in both knowledge and thought, that they would never have to set foot upon such a miserable place.

And then one day a ship approached this horrid place, its crew unaware of what was about to become of them, for the Zuytdorp had ventured too close to land....

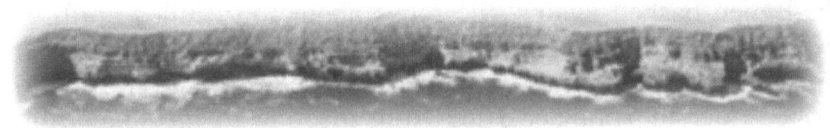

PROLOGUE

The Swan River Colony was founded in 1829, a community no different than any other found on the east Australian coast. The land was bountiful, gifts ready for the plucking. The name Swan River was derived from that which it was christened, by the Dutch, many decades before, when black swans upon the river evoked a stirring of affection and beauty within the men that saw them. So beautiful they were that several were taken back to the Netherlands as somewhat of a gift to the people and the government.

It was just five short years after this 'founding' when two aboriginals could be seen within the district, walking with such a leisurely pace that they seemed to carry but not a single worry, not a single hurt within them; not a care in the world.

They were Tonquin and Weenat, tall men of darkened flesh, rather beautiful when it comes down to the point of characteristics. Their faces were alive, a living script to the lives they had so-far lived. The very structure of the skin and bone, their faces of undulating skin and large noses that appeared to sit flat and a little crooked, were but testimony to a life well lived, a life shared with nature and what the land had to offer them.

They had come to terms with the white men from afar, the way in which they settled upon the land, and wondered what they could do in order to share common courtesy, where food and tobacco might replace their friendly gesture and information on the shipwreck that had come their way. Such information must be worth something for it was a white man's ship, one that had been bashed against the rocks about forty miles north of Kalbarri. But the information they had was somewhat misconstrued, hazy to say the least, passed down from tribe to tribe, elder to young, carried from meeting to meeting, from corroboree to sacred ceremony.

The police officer sat rigid behind his desk before relaxing a little, listening with great effort to the story pressed upon him, the sentences delivered his ears missing words here and there, but the main gist of the story was noted for what it was. There was a shipwreck some thirty days walk to the north in the land of the Malgana, where the tribe Wayle lived off the land in pleasant solitude.

There was much money that had been washed upon the rocks, silver coins that were so thick in the water that it was ankle deep in places. The ship had broken up into three main parts, a three-mast ship that no longer resemble anything more than the remnants of a pile of rubble in places, covered by ocean waves.

Tonquin and Weenat looked the officer up and down as he took his notes, writing upon a sheet of paper the points that he needed to remember the most. They then continued with their story of how the tall white men were taken in by the aboriginals, where courtesy was exchanged with courtesy; and the relationship between the two became good.

The officer displayed a frown, missing a little of the interpretation, thinking that the wreck had just recently occurred, not considering for a moment that the information being delivered to him was 122 years old.

And further still, both Tonquin and Weenat advised that the white men lived in little houses, around three fires, each made of wood and canvas, and not so very far from the face of the cliff.

The police officer decided that he must act quickly, provide aid to those in need, and so a rescue was prepared, a rescue that was 122 years too late, and nothing would be found of any survivor - unless one was to dig and conduct a thorough examination of the site.

CHAPTER ONE

Today, the 5th of June, 1712, and on board the Zuytdorp are 286 souls: 174 seamen including those of higher rank, 100 soldiers, 4 tradesmen and 8 passengers. Almost all will perish.

It came upon the men, women and children without warning, a great calamity that fell upon them in the dark of the night. The sky above was as dark as one had ever known it, only intermittent sparks of light throwing themselves upon the world and decking around as lightning struck its cord with the savagery of wind and rain.

The thunder rolled all around them as the wind stole their breath away, little voice being herald to safe ear, for the strength of the gale broke up the shouts for all to pull their weight, remnants of garbled speech not being heard. Crew members on deck however were throwing themselves to duty as though it were the last thing they would ever do, and it would be the last if they were not successful in their endeavours.

The eight passengers below deck huddled together, bound by the horror which had culminated their fear to the highest point in this journey of theirs to Batavia. Their sight of the situation fared a little better as several small oil lamps were alight, swaying back and forth as the ship rocked like a cork in a tub. Three were wives heading to Batavia, a child in each of their arms, upon a voyage to lay visits upon husbands and fathers of high and important stations. The other was a man, neither brave nor cowardly, neither weak nor strong. He was heading to Batavia to fill a position advertised back at home, a position which would see the skills of his profession as a bookkeeper taxed to the limits. And there was one other, a child of fourteen, older than the others cradled safely close to mothers' breasts, and he was alone; in fact, the only keeper he had was the bookkeeper, for the bookkeeper had sworn to maintain a vigil on the boy during the long and frightful journey.

The boy's name was Willem Steyns, cast upon whichever way the wind would carry him, to take him far and wide until the limits of the earth had been reached; or so it seemed. He had been set forth by a poor mother, a drunken wretch worthy of nothing except the little money she carried in her purse. He had been cast aside by her, for him to be attended to by his father, a merchant in Batavia, and a man of lean living and completely unaware of the poor state in which his wife of England had founded for herself. In fact, he wasn't even aware that Willem was on his way to seek him out for the letter his wife did dispatch was carried by the boy himself.

The man, as tall as he was fair, tried with all his might to comfort the small group of seven as the calamity above deck continued unabated, fifty per cent of the crew seeking to right what was wrong and to ensure that the ship they sailed upon would see the light of day once more. His name was Pieter Pelsaert, 34 years of age.

Pieter had come to know the three women and Willem rather well, having spent the entire voyage strapped to their every yarn and piece of gossip, heralded to hear of what they would say about the captain of the ship or a member of his crew. They were thrown together in an area away from the main body of seamen whose job it was to see them and the ship's cargo safely ported to dock in Batavia.

Pieter saw one of the women fall, atop her baby of just 14 months, its face as blue and crimson as any darkened sky and heated furnace. He helped her up then.

"My God," Pieter bellowed into the woman's ear as he pulled her up from the sopping floor. "What manner of transgression forced you to attend this voyage with one so young? What are you running from?"

He picked the two up and noticed soon enough that he had scolded her in the face, a torment which was yet to be fully revealed, for without realising it the woman sobbed as she looked at the man and then down into the lifeless eyes of the one she held in her arms.

Pieter's mouth dropped.

"My boy; he's dead," said Willemtgen. She looked down upon the form of flesh that she pulled into her, a tightened grip that could not be pried loose. The tears streamed from her face and Pieter put an arm around her and she shifted upon the floor. The other ladies looked upon the scene and then to their own young; Ariaantje with her 18 month old girl and Willemyntje with her 4 year old daughter.

Suddenly the door burst open and a seaman by the name of Ariaen Leyden looked into the parlour of darkness flaked with the fluctuating light of the lamps, shadows moving around abruptly as the Zuytdorp creaked and groaned, bellowed and cried.

"Pieter, quick man, we need you! All hands to deck, now Pieter!" and with more suddenness than the man had employed as he entered, the entire ship shuddered that unthinkable shudder, a noise from beneath her hull, and the entire vessel shifted on its axis, the stern trying with all its might to overtake the bow by moving out to the port. She had hit a rocky seabed that loans no remorse.

She first hits rock at one hundred and twenty feet from the shoreline platform, a platform which is dwarfed by the cliff either side. It is swivelled around parallel to the coast, stern to north-west, and bow to south-east, driven sideways upon the shore of rock upon rock, upon rock.

The fear within the eyes of the women were of the sheerest grief, their distorted faces of horror painting a picture of little doubt. Each clutched ever more the little ones so close to them, even Willemtgen embraced hers as though he was still full of life and vigour.

"We're going!" yelled Ariaen as he fell heavily away from the doorway, knocking his head heavily upon the mast of the ship that penetrated deep into the Zuytdorp, and with great ease and horrible wrenching the mast from just above the deck did snap and fell away with the rigging, the little sail currently on loan to the wind falling with it, tearing here and ripping there.

The Zuytdorp was under short sail and in the midst of an early winter storm. This big, square-rigged ship was unable to move effectively, and the pending disaster was unavoidable.

Men upon the deck were thrown overboard, presented to the mercy of the sea, but little mercy was received this night. Barrels and cannons rolled around the decking killing men as quickly as a trail of ants became trodden on by a heavy foot.

The cargo in the hold shifted suddenly, aiding the abrupt shifting of the Zuytdorp upon its current course, barrels and sacks of all variety, much of the merchandise tearing open for the rats below deck to avoid in their rush for safer quarters.

The Zuytdorp carried within her a great quantity of merchandise including precious metals, wealth in the form of silver coins being its largest hoard. Coins in their thousands; Dutch ducatons, guilders, rix dollars, schillings, double stuivers and stuivers; Spanish pieces of eight, pieces of four and pieces of two; Spanish-Netherlands ducatons and patagons. There was also Gold which came in the form of Dutch ducats and ingots of silver too. The great quantities of wealth were carried in chests, packed and secured to prevent movement. Two locks saw to it that each chest was bolted secure, each chest then nailed down secure with sail cloth within the captain's cabin below the poop; silver coins to the value of 248,886 guilders, 100,000 guilders of which were newly minted schillings and double stuivers. But she also carried other commodities; lead, linseed, bacon, needles, muskets and blunderbusses. She was filled to the brim with barrels of wine and beer; butter, 1,813 pounds of fresh meat, ten live sheep, vegetables, potherbs, 2 hundredweight of beans, 2 hundredweight of peas, 300 pounds of rice, bacon, oils, cloth, rope, sulphur, pitch, canvas, paper, leather, copper, salt, sail yarn, window panes, medical stores, iron hoops and plates. And what good was all of this? It was ambition, enterprise and above all money to be made. Not only was there wealth to be sanctioned from the hull of this grand ship but the Zuytdorp was to return to Europe with an even bigger catch; Spices, salt, pepper, textiles, china, cotton, silks, tea, coffee, nutmeg, cloves, cinnamon, mace, and anything else that could be tied down, or locked away in chests and barrels.

Damn it; damn it all. It was all loose, being thrown around here and there; impossible to avoid whether below deck or upon it. Men were being killed. Broken bones made their appearance; broken arms, broken noses, and a sudden call was snatched by the wind, a call of 'every man for himself', and no sooner had it be called then the man responsible was speared in the gut by flying debris as another of the ship's masts snapped and fell upon the decking, the ship pitching further off its bearings and being forced upon the unforgivable shoreline of rock.

The Zuytdorp gave way to sudden bouts of lurching, enormous waves of terror thrashing out upon the starboard side of the ship, water commencing to flow freely within the hull, the vessel taking on water, everyone trying with all their effort to save themselves from the torments of the sea. It was not a time to reflect upon anything except all manner of escape, but one thing was clear within every single one of those still alive and able to think, and that was that the ship was wrecked.

Pieter took this as a call for him to act, a call to duty which was not his to answer but the last thing he wished to do was leave anyone behind, in particular an helpless woman with child, be it dead or alive, or the boy known as Willem.

"Quickly, Willem; you have to help me," and Pieter stumbled with the shifting of the ship as it grinded itself upon the bottom, further groans of mayhem being voiced from the very fibre of the ship's core, wood commencing to split, the sound of cracking wood reaching their ears, so loud that it could hardly be believed.

"What do I do," came Willem's reply, the fright upon his face written in bold, the bulging eyes giving rise to the frantic state of his mind and nerve. "Tell me, Pieter."

Pieter could not deny that the boy's frame of mind scared him to wit's end, but the boy must be forced to endure and provide assistance, for only then would he forget the fear within him and commence to crawl from the abyss in which he had fallen.

"Give aid to Willemtgen and her son, I'll attend Ariaantje and Willemyntje," said Pieter in haste, as Willem's mouth began to open. "Quickly, now!"

"Please, Willemtgen," said Willem as he set to his task. "Take hold of my arm and we'll scale the steps together."

Willemtgen's face showed a glare of hope then, even with her dead son still in her arms, as she reached out to grab hold of the boy. It was just then that the worst thing that could possibly happen did occur.

The entire ship broke into three pieces as a huge wave with frightening force behind it hit hard the starboard side of the Zuytdorp. The bow broke away, 22 feet of her, and shifted 60 feet towards the shoreline platform where many large boulders with bone-breaking knobs and points awaited its delivery, to gnaw upon it as a man gnaws upon a bone. The stern headed in a forward motion towards the nearest portion of shoreline, just 28 feet away from the main bulk of the ship, breaking up just a little but steadying herself upon the rocks, 53 feet of her in which all the treasure on board was stowed. The centre most portion, all 85 feet of that which remained, rammed home against the platform, the fallen mast upon the deck crushing several men as it shifted position.

Those few men that remained upon, or within, the bow portion of the vessel, died quick and slow deaths, broken bones and concussion; drowning and knocked unconscious, trapped within the rigging and skewered by the wood of the ship, large splitters delivering death as though she, the Zuytdorp, was filled with a cursed evil. And those of the stern fared little better, the portion of the ship in which Pieter and Willem were housed, alongside their female companions and other members of the crew.

The higher the station a sailor of the sea held and the closer he could find himself to the door of the captain's quarters, and other than the captain himself were the following: the uppersteersman, senior carpenter, master surgeon, second carpenter, understeersman, comforter of the sick, third carpenter, undersurgeon, clerk, master gunner and bosun; the stockmaker, bricklayer, coppersmith and firelock maker... all were dead, spread out through the ship, cast out upon the sea, dashed upon the rocks of the coast, pulled beneath the waves by the surmounting weight of wave upon wave as they crashed upon their victims without a shred of effort or remorse.

But Pieter broke free from the ferocity of the sea as it swelled in upon him, spluttering and gasping for breath as he tried with all his effort to gain some form of initiative against his predicament. He saw a baby floating close by and then the body of a woman, and then another, and finally the third. And Willem suddenly clawed his way from the bottom, breaching the surface of the sea with an outstretched arm reaching for the sky. They were surrounded on three sides by the interior of the ship which they had called home, the fourth side was now wide open to the dark night air. And with as much astonishment as they could perceive the glory of God cast down upon them the opportunity of a lifetime, the hands of glory pushing aside a small opening in the sky, just enough to allow a little light to make its way down to earth, to light up the scene around them. With the accompaniment of the lightning strikes the two, both man and boy, could see one another and the silhouette of the cliff that looked like doom peering down upon them.

"Are you okay, Willem? Are you hurt!" shouted Pieter at the top of his lungs, the open side of the stern becoming an open invitation for more noise to envelope them both.

"Yes; yes! I'm okay," came the reply and Pieter moved closer to the boy, the one he had grown a little fond of, the one that had kept him company on occasion and had lifted his spirits when they were down. Now it was Pieter's job to see to it that the favour was returned by saving the child's life and remaining by his side in this, their hour of need. Pieter, the bookkeeper, was to fulfil his duty as carer, to provide all the support he could to the boy of fourteen.

There was a small gap between the stern and the shoreline, the platform of rock which was vacant of sand. There was no soft landing, no offering of support from nature. The gap had to be breached by them without their being thrust against the rocky talons of that which stood before them.

To speak more than what was required was wasteful. When gasps for air were called upon, and energy reserves within were the only means by which to climb to safety, all else mattered little. Instinct took over and together the two bodies of flesh and bone acted as one.

Pieter closed the small gap towards the boy and grabbed hold of his arm, each then reached for buoyancy which came in the form of a large piece of debris, and then an upturned barrel. But the barrel fell from their grip and filled with water. They grabbed hold of a chest, a foot locker with air trapped within it, offering to provide sufficient support for them to make their way towards the rocky platform which was now within view below the cracking brilliance of piercing light delivered by another lightning strike, different shades of darkness outlining the scene before them.

The energy within them peaked quite rapidly to such a degree that within as little as half a minute both found themselves so near the edge of the platform that they could almost touch it, the platform which was covered in crashing waves and ebbing surf. It was like being upon the surface of a giant cauldron at the boil, and without warning a tidal surge of water lifted them both up and over the danger of the jagged lip, a miraculous salvation from harm which they were most grateful for.

"Quickly! Willem; to me; grab my hand!" yelled Pieter, his voice penetrating the cold of the night where the wind and spray from the sea stung at his unprotected face.

Willem reached for Pieter, stretching beyond his doubt until fingertip touched fingertip and then their hands were clasped together like welded metal. Pieter pulled the boy to him and in the fury of gut-deep surges, where the platform made itself visible from time to time, its undulating surface offering itself as just another obstacle, the two scrambled to a temporary safe haven behind a large boulder: a small pinnacle or nubbin, being part of the rock formation itself.

The sea continued to lap up around them and another freak wave forced itself up and over their protection, the man and boy gasping for air as the water ebbed back into the fury of the sea in readiness for another opportunity to beat itself against the platform of rock and the Zuytdorp.

Pieter looked up and saw his opportunity for salvation, a rampart of sorts, a mass of crumbling rock, detritus in all its glory which was steep but passable; rock, stone and boulders having fallen away from the cliff, a way to the summit of the cliff face before him being revealed, the height of the cliff still obscured from knowledge due to the inaccuracy of perception in the current light and surrounding misery.

"Willem; with me; come with me, now," ordered the tall bookkeeper, and together they scrambled up the gradient of detritus as best they could, losing two steps to every three that they took but making such good progress considering the position and condition that they were both in.

Each must have slipped at least ten times in the short trek to the top, their fingernails splintered, caked in mud, cuts and abrasions upon their skin, muscles torn in the effort applied. There was not a single part of their body which was not working itself hard; all the tissue, ligaments, muscle; both physical and mental; all was worked to the brink of collapse. Every thought but that of survival was shaken from their minds as they continued on up the slope.

Salvation wasn't far ahead, they could see and feel it, looking up momentarily to see what was ahead, to try and visualise how far they needed to climb before victory was won. And on reaching the top a little more cloud moved aside and more light lit up the night as both of them fell onto all fours at the edge of the cliff, exhausted beyond all realisation, Pieter and Willem then collapsing upon the rock of the cliff that was little more than 115 feet high.

They gasped for air where they lay, a great wave of relief empowering both to sit up and look around, both open mouthed and in disbelief, shock taking momentary hold prior to another surge of adrenalin embracing the sanity they still had within them.

It was now, with the providence offered them that they could see out across the scene of destruction, the Zuytdorp ripped apart into three main parts, her cargo spread far and wide, planks of wood being thrown through the air alongside barrels and other matter, each a lethal weapon that lashed upon the unwary. But what could they do? These two skeletons of humanity, starved in the course of the voyage, tired from the conditions on board ship, tired from the swim to shore, the climb to higher station, and exhausted beyond all imagination.

There was nothing they could do for the others, those below in the surf, still aboard ship and attempting to pull themselves to safety and away from harm.

Many men could be seen, dashed against rocks, hit hard by an unsuspecting barrel, drowned by the viciousness of a wave and the surges of water coming down upon them one after the other without a moment's stay.

"Hey, up here; we're up here!" shouted Willem as he waved his arms in a frantic attempt to help those below, the rain falling hard upon him, stinging at his numbed face, the pain hardly felt due to the calamity of the situation.

Pieter lifted an arm and made Willem lower his by grabbing a gentle hold of his wrist.

"Save yourself, Willem," said Pieter with angel eyes looking upon the boy of fourteen, the boy looking back, their stares locked momentarily. "They can't see nor hear you."

"Then what are we to do, just sit here and do nothing?"

"Avert your eyes, Willem. That's all you can do," advised Pieter.

"But we must do something to help."

Pieter looked down upon the scene and then back to the boy who he could see was now in fact a man.

"Then do as I do, Willem. Keep your eyes open. Ignore the pain you see; ignore the horrors of this night, of the devil at play.

Watch, Willem; watch with your entire might and keep a mental record of where people lay. Keep a note on where they may be found on the break of this viciousness in order for us to venture down and pull all ashore. There will be survivors, Willem, as we have survived, but all we can do now is watch... but ignore the suffering you see, do not allow their suffering to plague your mind."

And Willem nodded acceptance of the task set before him and both cast their eyes upon the horrors of the shipwreck as it continued to develop into a betrayal that was cast down from heaven above, and the cold of the storm penetrated deep, the panic that had overridden the effect of the cold having dissipated. He began to shiver.

"Here, Willem," said Pieter. "Sit in front of me, between my legs. We can gain a little warmth." He looked around into the dark and saw nothing behind him but frequent exposures of an open land with no apparent cover available.

"I see nothing at all," continued Pieter. "Nothing but open ground." Willem was now seated in front of the man. "We must remain strong; stay as warm as possible until the storm has abated. From our experiences on ship I think I can safely surmise that this cold spell is not something that is common for this land."

"I've heard many stories," said Willem as his teeth chattered and his body convulsed a little with shudders of pain, "that this land is as cold in the winter months as it is hot in the summer."

"No one has been around long enough to tell the difference," voiced Pieter above the storm and thrashing waves from below, spray from the sea reaching them with little difficulty. "This job of ours will be a hard one," added Pieter. "I don't know if we should remain aloft the wreck for too long. I feel the pain of this bitter cold within you as I feel it within me, you there, shivering like a nervous wreck." He looked around himself once more.

"Willem; I don't think we'll find adequate shelter but we can't remain here. We must find a hollow in the least, something to shelter us from the wind."

Without a further word the two stood up, and stooped lower than normal proceeded away from the cliff face and into the unknown.

It wasn't long before they came across a small re-entrant, a small stream with banks of little concern. They followed this for some distance before coming upon a band of scrub; thick and seemingly impenetrable.

"Maybe we should turn back," said Willem with growing concern.

"Up here, Willem. I see several boulders. Come; follow me."

They stepped out of the low ground and halted next to several large rocks, and behind them, away from the blast of the wind and soaking of the rain, sought shelter for the remainder of the night, curled up and holding each other close. They did not sleep whilst the storm continued in its fury, but the rest they attained was better than nothing at all, their thoughts on any possible survivors and how they would be able to help come morning.

By the time the storm had blown itself clear of the coast the sun was almost upon them, and it was at this time that they fell asleep.

CHAPTER TWO

Birdsong was filling the air from some distance away, a medley of choruses that seemed to have suffered little, uninhibited by the night's misery, and as the mellow sounds from many species filled the air the two fragile forms of human existence woke up to be greeted by the arrival of the sun. The bite of the cold was easily felt upon them, though now there was not a cloud in the sky, and the cold of the morning had less effect on them than the night before, where they were covered in the spray of the ocean and rain from the sky; but with their clothes still being very wet and their combined body heat less effective than they would have liked, the chill teased them when they moved from their tight embrace.

Willem was the first to sit up and was followed shortly by Pieter, both shivering and fighting to open their heavy eyelids.

Suddenly a vibration hit them both, a sound unfamiliar and a long way off, a penetrating sound that was mystifying to say the least.

"Did you hear that, Pieter?"

"I did, Willem," the man answered as he stood up upon his feet, looking out towards the north-east, from where the sound made its unwavering approach. "And I think I know what it is."

"What?" asked Willem as he looked up into the tall man's eyes, seeing the reflection of humanity still alive in the sodden form that stood before him, a man with scratches and bruises covering his arms and face, his clothes torn and tattered, his trousers ripped down one entire side baring the flesh of his leg to the world, his shoes missing and socks soaked.

"I think it's the men of this world."

"Wretched souls of humanity," replied Willem, casting his eyes upon the earth.

"There has been much talk; much hearsay, which may be untrue," corrected Pieter.

"Do you think they'll eat us?"

A small smile caressed Pieter's face, "No. But let's forget that for the moment. We must get back to the cliff, view the damage, and find what survivors we can."

Leading the way back to the cliff face, Pieter looked behind him from time to time during the short trek to ensure that Willem was close by and at hand, and before they knew it they were stepping up towards the edge of the cliff and looking down upon the site of the shipwreck.

Such a site could never be explained; the feelings of despair and depression, the horror of seeing the bodies lying upon the now exposed platform of rock. There was debris everywhere, not a single foot of ground bare to a part of the wreck, be it a plank of wood, a barrel, cannon, cloth or body. Every single item of commerce transported within the Zuytdorp seemed to be free of its holdings, splashed upon the scene as though in reckless doubt, doubt as in whether to stay or be swept out to sea, the former glory of the ship itself torn apart into three parts, each wedged up tight against the shoreline platform. It was sheer misery that enveloped them both and as they perused the tragedy a voice came from behind them.

"Pieter, is that you?" asked a weary voice, a man by the name of Ariaen Leyden.

The bookkeeper turned, half startled to death by the broken silence.

"My God, Ariaen; thank God... you're alive," said an exuberant Pieter, stepping towards the man of 28 years, a man of the sea, a common sailor who had made the voyage to Batavia on three separate occasions as well of many years travelling between the countries of Asia under the keeping of the VOC.

"I'm well."

And from behind the man came further hope, a mass of people, twelve all told, each as weathered as the first, dressed as lepers, steeped in rags, and a majority without footwear upon their feet, feet that had been lacerated by rocks. Some of those present were in shock, had been soaking wet all night long, cold from the early winter storm and the face of the wind.

"How many of you are there?" asked Pieter.

"We're seventeen, including me, but several of them are injured."

"What kind of injuries? Asked Pieter as those from behind Ariaen closed the gap, sunken faces worn by them all, the life gone from their eyes like the embers disappear from the remnants of a blazing fire, turning stone cold as on a winter's morning.

"Broken bones, mostly; and some of the walking, as you can see behind me, carry many cuts and abrasions."

Pieter looked upon his friend and saw a gash on his forehead, a deep wound that had clearly removed some bone.

"You too are hurt."

"It appears so. It hurts like hell to tell you the truth but there is more suffering here today than could ever be suffered by me in a lifetime of suffering."

"We need to move down to the wreck," started Pieter before looking upon the others and raising his voice, "to the wreck we must go, to look for survivors; others that may be trapped and require our assistance."

"No, Pieter," said Ariaen. "We've been down there already, me and two other men. We've searched everywhere and not another soul has survived."

"Are you sure...? Maybe you missed someone; maybe there is hope left for some unfortunate soul left stranded below this cliff."

Ariaen grabbed his friend upon the upper arms, "No, Pieter. We've tried. There is no one else."

"Then what's to be done?"

"Supplies. We need water the most. Drinking water and food; bandages and medicine for the sick. We need tools for cutting splints."

"And a cannon," voiced Cornelis Lieffers, a young man of 19 years, and a seaman of vast experience for having joined the VOC so young, "to signal a passing ship."

"Shoes," voiced another from behind, "we also need shoes."

Pieter looked down at the man's feet and then to his own. Yes, indeed, there was much to be sought.

Pieter looked to the others and quickly realised that they were like lambs, flocking around a single soul. It seemed that Ariaen had adopted the leadership role for all concerned but Pieter felt he had more to offer.

"I am a bookkeeper and some of you know me. I have exercised my ambition and expertise upon many stations of the sea and visited many ports, all of this before my 29th birthday when, soon after, I decided upon remaining sure-footed and comforted upon dry land. In time I grew to change once more and decided to work elsewhere. I have many degrees and sound knowledge on navigation. It would honour me if you'd all allow me the opportunity to help in this predicament of ours."

A man took a few steps forward and the others around him also stirred, "I am Hendrik Blaauw. Ariaen knows me. I am 47 years old and have spent most of my life upon the sea. Why should the task of command and rescue go to one as you?"

"I have—."

"Yes, yes; you have degrees," Hendrik announced sarcastically as he turned to look at the others around. "Does a common piece of paper hold more authority than experience?"

"I am simply offering my hand," said Pieter in defence. "It's for you to decide what to make of it."

"I say that we make-of-it right now," voiced Hendrik. "Who shall be in command of this shipwrecked crew? Let's vote!"

"Aye!" shouted one; "here, here," came another.

"All of those in favour of me taking command place your hands up in the air," commanded Hendrik.

With Ariaen and his twelve, then Pieter and Willem, there stood to be cast a total of fifteen votes, from there upon that very spot.

Eight hands showed themselves after a little hesitation, including Hendrik's.

"The tally has spoken," said Hendrik. "I have eight votes, including mine; the remaining seven will be yours."

"What of the lame, the ones with broken bones?" asked Ariaen in defence of his trusted friend. "Don't they have a vote?"

"I have spent many years at sea and know that gangrene will visit them all. A dead man can't vote."

Ariaen then considered the situation, instantly deciding upon something more: "And what of me?" stated Ariaen. "I wish to make a stand. I am from a higher station than most."

"There's no rank here," came a voice from the back.

"That's right," confirmed Hendrik. "We're no longer on the sea. Our survival depends on being able to live off the land until a ship comes to the rescue."

"Which won't be long now," said Ariaen to all those listening to the argument unfold. "I know that the Kockenge will pass by these shores soon... within the week. When we were at Table Bay I also heard of others. We can expect such ships as the Oostersteyn, the Zuyderbeeck, Belvliet, Popkensburg, Corsloot and the Oude Zyp; all of these to come past this way over the next four to five weeks. Not all will be seen by us; not all will come within range to our waving arms. We need to build a signal fire and prepare it for immediate ignition when the time is right... we need to get a cannon," said Ariaen as he lay his eyes upon Cornelis Lieffers, the 19 year old with the idea to save them all. "We must bury the dead and collect rations where possible, and much, much more."

"Here, here," yelled Dirck Fret from the rear. "All those that vote for Ariaen put your hand in the air," and to the astonishment of Hendrik a show of nine hands could be seen, including those of Willem and Pieter.

"Not counting the soon-to-be-dead," added Pieter to the insult.

"So let it be done," said Hendrik in defeat, the evil in his eyes brewing something against what appeared to be nothing less than a conspiracy against him, ignoring the comment against those injured by the storm, by allowing them a vote.

CHAPTER THREE

The storm had done its job well, the pounding surf having smashed the hull, driving it into shallow water three to ten feet deep beside the shoreline platform.

It was easy to see how many of the survivors had reached safety, a large tangle of rigging alongside a fallen mast connecting the ship with the shore. It was precariously unstable at the moment and wouldn't stay long where it currently lay. It was a devastating site and beyond belief.

The cliff was limestone and only around 90 feet high at the actual wreck site. The area before the cliff was a jumble of boulders and jagged rock, no sand. The stretch of rock before the cliff was approximately 65 feet wide and 6.5 feet above sea level.

To all of those now looking upon the scene, from atop the smallest portion of cliff along the entire coast [for 155 miles], an unbroken stretch of cliff disappeared into the horizon; so daunting to say the least, it was nothing less than a devastating blow to morale.

A carpet of silver could be seen far below, glimmering in the early morning sunlight, every single chest of treasure seemingly revealed to the world. The biggest decision was where to start.

"We need to be systematic about our salvage," announced Ariaen as all of those present gathered around. "I see the wonder in some of you, the glittering of the silver below lighting up your eyes. Listen to me; the money will do nothing for you if you're dead. It'll all still be there next week and the week after that.

Help yourself if you wish but remember one thing; whatever you salvage of the silver is the property of the VOC and when we're rescued it will have to be returned. You'll receive no special favour, so leave it. Some of you need shoes; that is priority. We need wood for shelter, a cannon if possible, just the one will serve our purpose. Breech blocks will help the most, the more we can salvage the better. Food and fresh water, barrels for storage and anything else you think appropriate. This is the calm after the storm and we don't know what the future holds. We may not get another opportunity to gather supplies so let us make the most of it."

Ariaen then waved his hand frantically about his face, trying with great effort to release himself of the bondage that the flies around him had subjected him to... there were thousands of them.

There were nods of agreement and the men commenced to lower themselves towards the platform, slipping upon the steep bank as they made for what remained of the good ship Zuytdorp.

Little was said during the task, shoes being pulled from the dead, bodies collected and moved towards the cliff where they could be pulled to dry land by ropes and rigging, for the corpses would rot and create all manner of disease and if the shipwreck was to be made a constant visiting pleasure for those in search of different items then the threat of disease must surely be extinguished... besides, didn't the dead also deserve a decent burial.

Several men tried to get one of the smaller bronze swivel guns ashore along with the breech blocks for it, guns mounted on the poop deck, the highest part of the ship and currently quite accessible. Eight breech blocks altogether were taken ashore but the swivel guns were too cumbersome and heavy, unable to be moved. No other guns could be taken ashore.

The breech blocks were 12-18 inches high, weighing approximately 28 pounds each and looked remarkably like large jugs, drinking cups with handles, and a pair of callipers were also taken ashore along with brass dividers to aid in navigation should they later decide to make a boat in an effort to launch it and make for Batavia, even though no map was secured from the wreck.

Others concentrated on gathering food and it wasn't beyond Willem, of all those that were scampering around looking for salvage that would be of some use, to find that the area was encrusted with oysters, abalone, whelks, periwinkles, rock barnacles, mussels and other shellfish. Whether or not they could survive solely upon shellfish was another concern, something that Willem was too young to consider... and how long would the supply last the totally-combined, nineteen survivors, especially in the face of the impending difficulty where many were on the brink of gangrene and death?

One of the searchers found dry powder for a musket, but no musket, and sheets of lead, and all manner of the wreck was deposited upon the base of the cliff and out to where the wreck lay in three parts. A figurehead of a pregnant women had been dislodged from the Zuytdorp and thrown against rocks, this was carried into a cavern below the cliff face for safe keeping, too large to worry about carrying to the cliff top at present as there were more important things to do, the figurehead a possible memento of little worth other than a reminder that could be made into a memorial of some description when the time was right. The figure was from the stern of the ship; she had a small plump face and bore a placid expression; she was the only woman amongst them, though mute and carved of wood.

One by one, in their two's and three's, men appeared briefly upon the cliff top to place down their salvage before returning to the work; bodies too were accumulated on the platform below, stacked precariously, shoes taken by those that needed them, a quick prayer accompanying the removal of the footwear.

The ship's sails were torn apart – what was left of them – and taken to those with broken limbs, several men providing their special ability to give aid to the suffering, knowing a little on the subject of broken bones. It was a horrid sight, frantic yells for help reaching for the sky, even after the administering of alcohol, for many green bottles, square in shape and full to the brim with gin, were handed out willingly to those in need.

Some of the more fragile-of-mind, sought to carry many bottles off to a station upon the cliff face overlooking the sea. Here sat Gerrit Jongbloet, Jacob Albertsz, Jacobus Nuyts and Cornelius Brouwer. They had wandered off from their duty not long after it had commenced, drawing their bottles close into their chests, wrapping their arms around the necks of the bottles and caressing them as though they were wives. They suckled off the bottles as though being milked by their mothers, weaning the glass bottles of every drop, becoming drunk and loud amidst the misfortune that had fallen upon them all.

The four men with broken limbs lay not so far away, clutching at their ears to prevent the awful sound, for the drunken slander of those above the cliff face were as horrid as the screams that were emitted by those with broken bones.

Dirck Fret, 35 years old, and Wiebbe Leuftink, 29 years old, assisted those in need, the strain of their task being very real and unparalleled. Never before had either of them provided medical assistance without the aid of someone of sufficient knowledge beside them, but for what they achieved the victims were most grateful. But this, the degradation of the drunken swines not so far away, making a mockery of the survival situation; it was beyond belief. The two men could only look over their patients and talk to them with passion as the gin took its effect and the pain from their injuries commenced to evaporate for a while.

Francisco Roelofsz had a broken leg and a punctured gut

wound, Johannes Snitquer a broken arm and fractured skull, Marinus Leynsen had a broken arm and several broken ribs, and Hayman Jorisz had two broken legs.

Dirck looked to Wiebbe as the noise from the drunks drifted upon the breeze to where they had set up temporary shelter for the wounded, several planks tied together by rope and some of the ship's sail placed over the top of this to act as shade and protection from the wind and rain. It wasn't the grandest attempt anyone had made at pitching a shelter but for the time they had been allowed they fared reasonably well.

Out of earshot, Dirck said to Wiebbe, "I fear that Hayman won't last the week. He's in much pain and by morning the gin would have lost its effect."

"Hmmm," acknowledged Wiebbe. "I fear for Francisco. I'll go and see Ariaen, and ask him what he thinks."

"Don't give him too much credit, Wiebbe. He's just a man like us. Give him too much satisfaction and his position of command will go to his head."

"Then will be the time to change the leadership of this group," said Wiebbe and moved off without further word from Dirck being voiced.

Dirck pulled a sopping piece of cloth from a damaged bucket and wiped the sweat from Johannes' forehead, the bruising upon his skull being very evident, a large swelling and mostly red. There was much pressure beneath the skull and the worst was feared for his well-being, for his fever was very strong.

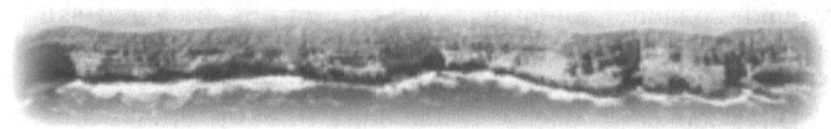

CHAPTER FOUR

Wiebbe approached Ariaen who had just appeared at the lip of the cliff carrying one end of a plank, Pieter coming up from the rear. They placed the plank down, and Willem, waiting patiently for his chance to perform his duty, lifted one end of the plank and pulled it with great effort over to a pile that he had growing rather large.

"The boy works well," noted Wiebbe, smiling at the boy and waving away flies.

"He's a man now," said Ariaen, seeing Willem's mouth erupt into a smile.

Wiebbe reflected briefly on the boy before announcing his reason for his running errand.

"The wounded are in a bad way... as I have said, the gin worked well but won't last the whole night. There'll be much suffering tonight."

"What about those drunken bums over near the cliff?" asked Pieter. "Can't we seize the bottles they have, give them to those in need?"

"Oh, they have more than you think," added Wiebbe. "They've taken a great quantity of bottles and have them close at hand; some hidden and others beside them."

"Take them," said Pieter as he looked to Ariaen and then Wiebbe.

"They have knives..." commenced Wiebbe. "What is it to us that they choose to crawl inside a bottle; really?"

"Inflicted by the devil. It will be to their own demise," said

Pieter.

"What is it that we can do for you anyway?" asked Ariaen.

"The wounded, as I have said; they're all in a bad way, but some more than others. Most of us have something to remember the storm by, but those four... I think their time is short. Francisco has a punctured gut as well as a broken leg. We can't do anything for the wound except bandage it. It will become infected soon unless it can be cleaned and closed."

"Can we attain anything from the ship's doctor?" asked Pieter of Ariaen.

"His cabin isn't far from the captain's. You were in there, Pieter. What was it like?"

"Last night it was like hell; this morning I searched for some personal belongings but found nothing. Most of the quarters are below the surface and I would hazard a good guess that the cabinet in which the medicine is kept would have been spoiled as much by the storm as the medicine would have been spoiled by the sea and rocks. I don't think we'll find anything there."

"Isn't it worth a try?" asked Wiebbe.

"I'll have another look," volunteered Pieter, none too confident that anything would come of the effort, and to that he was correct, for nothing could be salvaged from the doctor's belongings or the medicine under his charge.

"Meanwhile the only alternative is to comfort them," said Ariaen.

"And with that I'll return to my station," concluded Wiebbe.

Another man then appeared upon the cliff, a regular seaman as ever could be found. Jan Wysvliet put down an empty bucket and Willem came in from the side and removed it to his stockpile.

"Jan, can I ask something of you?" queried Ariaen.

"Certainly. What is it?"

"Take another man with you and find a campsite, somewhere

not too far away from the cliff but far enough to be away from the drunks over by the cliff just there."

"Sure," acknowledged Jan, tired reflection showing upon his face and the way in which he held himself. "I'll take Harmen with me."

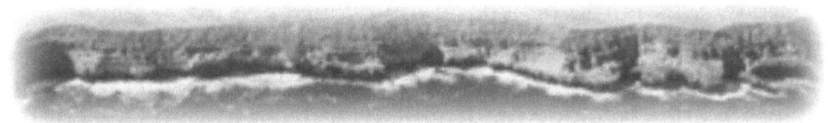

CHAPTER FIVE

Harmen Akkerman and Jan pushed themselves on into the unknown, and having quickly established a site for a camp, where the waters of the Indian Ocean could be seen both far and wide, decided to continue with their reconnaissance, for it wasn't enough for these two men of the sea to be satisfied with such a small accomplishment.

They commenced upon their reconnaissance of the area, in particular towards where they had heard the same sound that Pieter had heard earlier that morning, the flies going along to keep them company, thick upon their backs, licking at the saturation upon them both.

From the edge of the cliff inwards for about 1,300 feet was void of anything except a little low heath vegetation but after that there existed very dense scrub for two miles, made up of tea-tree and eucalyptus. The trees themselves were well spaced and would provide ample opportunity for the making of a small raft or shelter should the need arise; as it was, however, there was plenty of salvage from the wreck that would currently serve all of their purposes, including material for a fire, once the planks had dried sufficiently.

The going was tough on the men for they were already exhausted from the salvage operation, not to mention that they had gone without food passing their lips since the day before, but they continued on. The sky was a beautiful blue and there was not a cloud to be seen. Both felt as though winter was fast approaching the area, if not already in place, and felt that the clear sky was not to be a common occurrence over the coming months.

Several gullies presented themselves, each several hundred meters apart, stretching out from the land and towards the coast, being quite deep and several miles long. Like small streams during winter after heavy rain but dry for the remainder of the year. Harmen and Jan knelt down and drew handfuls of fresh water into their mouths, the tiny trickle of water from the night's storm refreshing them of what they had lost, the feeling lasting them for just a few minutes.

Small rock holes were also found to hold up to 12 gallons of water but these were scarce and not altogether a reliable source of water. It would seem that they would make a good source during the winter months only.

Further inland there was a great expanse of undulating sandplain stunted with low scrub, like a sea dotted with acacias, eucalypts and banksias. To these men of the sea, used to the sights and smells of home, where land was bound by cities in their fullest glory, the scene before them was devastating to say the least. The heat of the afternoon had built up quite dramatically, as it does at sea on long voyages, and their feet were swelling up with the effort of the walk, even though winter had well and truly started and the migration of some birds was already complete.

As they continued on into the clearing, Harmen came to a stop.

"Look, Jan. Over there," said Harmen, pointing with his head low as though trying to aim his finger with great accuracy, as though it were a weapon ready to be discharged.

"What do you see?" asked Jan as he looked off into the distance.

"A head, I'm sure of it. It moved, look... there it is again!" Harmen said hurriedly.

"Ah; yes. I see it too. It's not moving now. It has great ears and a long snout."

"A dog," concluded Harmen.

"No," disagreed Jan, looking his friend with lowered eyebrows, signifying his puzzlement at such a stupid suggestion. "Look around you, Harmen. This grass is almost chest high in places. If that is a dog then it'll be the largest damn dog I've ever seen."

"It could be standing upon a recent kill, or a dirt mound, searching for prey," suggested Harmen.

And then it moved, dashing off in leaps and bounds, against the open plains of grass-filled expanse, a kangaroo as never seen by the eyes of a white man before. Harmen and Jan cowered in the long grass, holding palm to chest, the fright of the animal moving with such rapid action catching them completely by surprise.

"Did you see that?" asked Harmen, and then another fifteen animals picked up their heads and followed the previous.

"My God. I don't believe it."

"We must get back with the news, Jan."

"No, not yet," Jan looked at Harmen and saw the anxiousness within him. "They're just animals, Harmen. We should look further, beyond where they stood."

"But not too far, Jan. We don't want to get lost."

"Lost," scoffed Jan. "We just head west, simple as that. Come; let's look some more."

Before they knew it the day was drawing to a close, and by the end of the day they felt exhausted. There was no time for a meal of any sort... it was missed; the sun commenced to disappear over the horizon, their eyes watching that stunning sight, the appearance of a myriad of colours cast across the sky and the stars came out in all their glory, giving enough light for them both to see out in all directions. The cool night air was comfortable enough to keep them from freezing and the sounds of the night reached their ears, but still they huddled together like man and wife: it wasn't until the early hours of the morning that the vacuum of cold left by the evaporated heat of the day hit them hard. It was all new to them, completely strange. Being too tired the night before and in the midst of a ferocious storm, they had missed the chorus of songs offered by the bush. And then out of the distance, seemingly not as far as they first thought, came the sounds that reverberated across the land, a ceremony taking place upon this strange land, a tune of drumming notes that brought the fear within them to surface.

There could be cannibals in the area and they were mightily concerned.

CHAPTER SIX

The salvage operation had gone quite well and before the sun disappeared below the horizon, all that could be carried to the top of the cliff, before the waves moved it out to sea, had been moved. There was still a lot of material to be had but it wouldn't be going far; too heavy to be carried out by the waves or still attached, even if precariously so, to the main hulk of the Zuytdorp. All of the barrels of wine and beer, the butter, ten sheep, rice, bacon and oils had been lost, as too, were much of the other stores. They were fortunate enough to have rescued a little of the vegetable – namely peas – and cloth; rope, canvas, salt and plates; this and just 128 pounds of meat, over 1,600 pounds having been lost to the hungry sea or simply ruined beyond contemplation, and the last thing the survivors needed was illness adding to their ruin.

The meat had salt rubbed into it but even so wasn't expected to last long; they would need to make the most of what they had and early on, hoping to secure more food as the days unfolded before them.

The bodies of the dead had been piled as delicately as possible to one corner of the shoreline platform, ready to be moved over the next few days to a fire which they intended to build, a fire which would not only act as a point from which to cremate all the dead but to signal any passing ship that might be within range of the coast. With the calculations suggested of the ships in port at Table Bay, and of the ship that accompanied them from that harbour, it was quite reasonable for Kockenge to be past their way over the coming six to seven days; and all knew that she was a slower vessel than the Zuytdorp.

The four men, drunk and beyond comprehension, lay near the edge of the cliff, their sorrows drowned to the point where they were literally oblivious to anything that was going on around them. Empty bottles of gin sat around them, some broken, some in one piece.

Away from the drunks a temporary fire had been lit by way of several lamps full of oil and a tinderbox procured by Ariaen, for he secretly held within his possession a small tobacco box of dry tobacco and the fire-starter. But his secret did not last, for although the average seaman displayed little intelligence, they weren't halfwits incapable of summing an answer from two plus two. He had come clean with his possession of the tinderbox but remained tight-lipped in regards to the little tobacco that he carried, and until such time that a suitable device for smoking could be secured he would have to content himself with sniffing his moistened weed of delectable perfume. Water was then brought to the boil, for a dry satchel of tea had been found along with a single tumbler rescued from the captain's cabin, but the tea was too little for the handful of survivors; a large quantity of meat was also cooked within a pot found on the shoreline platform, enough to feed everyone present. The fire was heaven to them but wouldn't last. They hadn't gathered much wood and that which had been retrieved was still quite wet from the storm the night before. Pieter picked up the last of the lamps and shook it in inspection, seeing that it was quite empty. He stood up and threw it as far as he could towards the sea, temporarily jolted by the anger within him.

The injured had been moved to be right beside them in order for them to be provided assurance and comfort in their time of need, but it was too late for one. Johannes Snitquer, the man with the broken arm and fractured skull had passed away. His brain had hemorrhaged and death was like a dream, his thoughts fading away, drifting off to nowhere as he fell into a sleep from which he would not return. He was moved towards where the fire was to be built, a portion of the sail draped across him, for the blankets retrieved from the ship would serve a better purpose than to be discarded as a covering for the dead.

Seebaer Phillipse and Joannes Spandaun sat to one side of the small fire, talking between themselves and glancing at Ariaen from time to time. Ariaen responded.

"You have something to say," said Ariaen, kindly. "I see it by the way you are looking over at me."

Dirck and Wiebbe continued to examine the injured as the others shifted their eyes over to the two young friends, young seamen who were on their first voyage; never before had they been to sea.

"We think the fire should be bigger," answered Seebaer for the two. "No passing ship is going to see this... little thing."

"Have you been past this way before, in front of the coast of this strange land?" asked Ariaen as he rubbed his head wound, a thick broad bandage now covering his forehead and tied neatly at the side, courtesy of Wiebbe and his learning.

"We are both new to the sea," answered Seebaer as he shifted slightly upon his spot, a little embarrassed by his inexperience.

"I have been this way many times, and many times I have seen the shore from far out to sea," said Ariaen. "At this point, just off the coast, a ship will turn to the north and head towards its destination. Only during certain months of the year will one travel so far east that they will come into decent eye contact with this land. In all my time, traversing the coast from here and to the Sunda Strait, I have seen many fires. This land is inhabited by black men. They wear nothing upon their bodies and carry spears and shields. From my knowledge they are very ready for war and must skirmish with others from this land on a regular basis. A small fire will not do anything to encourage assistance of any description, but to do nothing will not satisfy everyone here. So I shall do as I think is best. When the dead are ready for burial and the fire built up as high as she can be built, we will cast a flame upon it and cremate all those that have perished... we can't bury them, there are far too many and we don't have the manpower or tools. I hope that the Kockenge will be near at that time to see something of our attempt to draw their attention to us but I don't expect it to be a success." Ariaen looked around the camp fire to all those that had survived, all except the drunks, and Harmen and Jan. "If we don't see a ship within the next five weeks then it will be time to consider our next move," a solid coughing spell then concluded his views on the subject, a fly being swallowed.

"What shall we do?" asked Seebaer.

"A ship arriving at Batavia will learn of our disappearance soon enough. It is possible that they might link our fire with those that are missing. I give it five weeks of signalling, conserving as best we can our fuel, linking our attempts to the time table I offered earlier. Ships will be past this way but their precise day of passing is simply a guess derived from what I heard before leaving Table Bay. After the fifth week we will wait until the approach of next summer and then make an attempt at launching our own boat, unless winter proves acceptable and not too ambitious. I have no idea at this stage how successful we will be... the first thing to do is find a good launching pad from which to set sail."

"I shall set out tomorrow," volunteered Seebaer. "I shall go south for one day and then return." He looked at his friend. "I'll take Joannes with me."

"Good," said Ariaen cheerfully. "Who will go north?"

Silence dominated the scene.

"Seebaer and I will go," volunteered Joannes, "once we've

returned from the south and have found... nothing."

"You may well find nothing, but even if you find something of value you should still take a look further afield," advised Pieter. "You might find something better in the north. And be sure to take some cooked meat, the driest portions; shellfish can also be obtained from the platform... if it extends that far south and north... and for God's sake, be careful."

Joannes nodded approval, "Very well. We shall look to the south and then the north."

"There are some blankets where Willem has been placing our stores. Take some with you," finished Pieter, Joannes nodding acceptance with a smile.

"Is there anything else that concerns anyone?" asked Ariaen. "I don't wish to command, as much as organise. We are all good seamen, even if young and out of our element for the first time, so no one here is any better than another, simply more experienced. It is this experience which we need to collaborate with in order to survive this ordeal."

The faces around the fireplace were filled with agreement for what was said.

Willem stood up and sat down again beside Ariaen.

"Shall I take some meat to the others?"

"You're a good lad, Willem... thinking of others when they have done no work this day."

"We shouldn't turn our back on them," said Willem. "I overheard one of the other men saying that they too wished they were drunk."

"Wishing to be drunk, and getting drunk, are two completely different things," said Ariaen, "but you give me an idea." He stood up. "We shall both deliver them some meat and whilst we are amongst them, if they appear incapable, or asleep as I expect, we will throw what they have of their stash into the sea."

"I'll come with you," said Hendrik. "Throwing evil drink into the sea will be my honour."

As expected the four drunk men were flat on their backs and sleeping heavily, drowned of all reality until the morning brought clarity to their pitiful lives once more. It took quite a while to find the spare bottles of gin that had been hidden, but in the stupor of their mindless action the four men had failed to hide their tracks and the source of their drunkenness was found. Willem too, enjoyed throwing the bottles as far as he could into the night air, the noise of the breaking waves upon the platform below a pleasantness that he hadn't expected, and on return to their fireplace they all drift off into sleep, a well-deserved rest from their arduous task being delivered and not for a second did they realise that the gin could have been used to their advantage when aiding the sick.

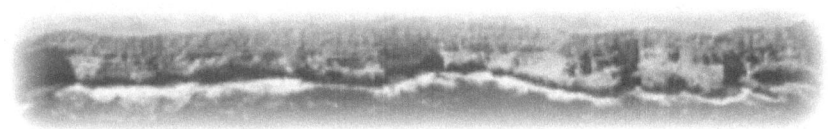

CHAPTER SEVEN

6th June, 1712.

None of the survivors awoke until the sun started to make its appearance. The day was a little cloudy but it was quite cold on this, their second morning in a strange land. It was at this same time that Harmen and Jan woke to be greeted by a noise in the bush not very far from their position.

Jan shook his friend and got up upon his knees, his head lifted high enough to see across the top of the expanse of grass, for as far as the eye could see, and where the grass died out there was nothing but a scorched earth to replace it, a prairie of softly undulating ground dotted here and there with eucalyptus to break up the monotony of the view.

"What is it?" asked Harmen as a rumble came from within him, rubbing his eyes as he spoke. "What do you see?"

"I don't know... my God! Quick, Harmen," yelled Jan, being up on his feet and running in the opposite direction as quickly as his feet could carry him.

The fright within Harmen was so high that his heart missed a beat and stole his breath for the briefest of seconds as he too shot up and looked out towards where Jan had glanced. There before him, just one hundred feet away, was a naked man with shield and spear, standing firm upon his ground and looking upon him as though mystified by the appearance, as though half astonished but unafraid.

Harmen was quick on his friend's heels and they continued at a fast pace for several hundred feet before coming to a stop and looking behind them, to see once again the dark flesh of the naked man looking upon them as though they were spirits from another world.

"Who do you think it is?" asked Harmen.

"I don't know and I don't care," answered Jan with scepticism taking strong hold upon him. "He's a savage; possibly a man-eater."

"Shall we try and communicate with him?"

Jan looked at the man as he stood there, some three hundred feet away and doing nothing but glancing in their direction.

"I think we should leave him be. There's no telling how many others are nearby," and with that said, Jan looked around to make sure that none other was trying to move to his rear, to cut off his withdrawal.

"I think he's alone," said Harmen.

"Yes, probably."

"He doesn't seem to be too concerned about us," added Harmen. "He has a weapon—."

"He's hunting for food," concluded Jan. "That creature we saw the other day, hopping across the ground in great stride." He looked his friend in the eyes. "The others won't believe any of it."

"Shall we return now?"

"Yes. Let's go and tell the others."

As they commenced the short journey back to the site of their misfortune they continued to shoot glances back over their shoulders to ensure that they weren't being followed, and although mightily concerned for the encounter which they had experienced, they didn't fail to take note of their surroundings.

Several gullies were crossed, the same as they had passed the day before. Several rock holes presented themselves for closer scrutiny, sources of water that would supply the survivors well over the coming months, and before long the undulating sandplain was well behind them and almost forgotten as the pair continued their painstaking walk back to the others, their stomachs feeling less empty than they had the night before, the pain of hunger dissipating slightly.

At around a thousand feet from the sandplains they came across a site which drew their attention.

It was on a higher elevation than the surrounding ground and reasonably good vigil could be maintained upon all directions even though the tea-tree scrub further afield prevented them from seeing the waters of the Indian Ocean.

There was an old camp fire and some bare spots where people had slept, and an old lean-to was laid flat upon the ground. A large tree provided shading and a large rock with a smooth concave surface – a grindstone made of basalt – sat next to the fire.

"It looks like our friend used this site," said Jan. "But it hasn't been used for a while."

"A summer camp," suggested Harmen. "That shelter isn't much to keep out the weather."

"Do you think he, or possibly they... that they'll return?"

"I don't know; but we'll have to keep an eye open," said Harmen as he moved over towards the fallen shelter where sheets of bark from the tree acted as part of the shelter. He bent down and lifted it up to see what else he could find. "Maybe they left some tools behind... a spear or something..."

"What is it...?" Jan said as he turned to the silence. He then froze.

Beneath the shelter, hiding coiled and peaceful beneath was a snake which was quick to lift its head and taste the air with its forked tongue.

Harmen had held himself well for the fright he had received, holding onto the shelter in his left hand and half stooped to look beneath the layers of bark. He was in easy striking distance of the reptile and quite at a loss as to what he should do.

The yellow scales of the six foot snake gave it a menacing look, not to mention the position it held, ready to lash out with a bite to Harmen's leg or arm.

Jan could see that Harmen wasn't going to move and considered the situation most briefly before arriving at a sound conclusion.

"I'm going to pick up a fallen branch, Harmen, to try and distract it. Don't move; for God's sake... keep still."

Jan moved around towards the rear of the snake, taking a long branch from upon the ground and preparing it for action. The snake turned its head to look upon Jan and as it did so, Harmen allowed himself to move his foot a little further from reach. Within an instant the snake turned and struck out at the movement, sinking its fangs into the flesh of the calf before retracting the dripping fangs and heading off into the scrub as Jan's empty effort to beat down upon it missed and he hit the hard earth instead.

Harmen bent over in more shock than pain, grabbing hold of the wound with the palm of his hand before removing it and taking a probing look with shaking fingers.

"Damn; damn that thing!" cursed Harmen as he fell upon his arse. "Of all the blasted luck. Shipwrecked upon this worthless land and now bitten by God knows what."

"I never saw such a thing," a shocked Jan said in reply, open-mouthed and looking out towards where the snake had slivered before turning his gaze upon the frightful look of his friend.

"What am I to do?" shrieked Harmen.

"The poison... we have to suck it out."

"Quickly," prompted Harmen. "Get a knife."

"I don't have one, Harmen."

"At the camp; get Dirck or Wiebbe," ordered Harmen.

"Quickly, Jan, or I'll die. Run for your life, get them, quick."

"Should you come with me? I can help by carrying you."

"No; but you're right... I can walk. Quickly; let's go."

Harmen got to his feet and started to run as fast as he could behind his friend Jan, running to be saved before the poison had time to react with his weakened body and spirit.

They weaved in and out of the scrub, pushing through the tea-tree which was very thick in places. There was more than a mile to go, over rough terrain and in a direction that was not guaranteed to bring them out on top of the others.

The sweat commenced to pour from them both as the water from the rock holes that had been drawn into their mouths through lips forming a tight circle, escaped their pores, and as the distance grew behind them, from the scene where the snakebite had occurred, Harmen suddenly halted and drew his hands to his heart. He fell suddenly like a sack of potatoes, straight to the ground in an instant, death overriding his will to live, a grotesque contortion painted upon his face.

CHAPTER EIGHT

Seebaer and Joannes had commenced their exploration of the south on morning's first light, taking nothing more with them other than some small portions of burnt meat procured from the meal the night before and a belly full of water. The intention was for them to return by last light, in this way they would be afforded a full stomach prior to setting out upon another exploration, this time to the north of the coastline.

The two had only travelled less than half a mile when they came across what appeared to be a small beach fronted by gentle sloping ground, which extended out onto a rocky sea floor. They took note of the area for the importance that it offered, not so much for the ability to launch a boat, in the case that they were able to make one, but for the sake of landing a boat from a rescue ship if one was to see their signal fire and come in close enough to the coast to rescue them.

They spent little time here as they were concerned in covering as much ground as possible and by midday their feet were rather tender; the effect of wet feet shoved either loosely or tightly into the shoes of its previous owner offering little comfort but much protection.

The way south, as too, was presumed for the north, was full of many species of wildlife, mostly of the feather, whistling, squawking, and fluttering upon the breeze. Creatures upon the ground were also numerous, with ants, centipedes, lizards and beetles foraging for food.

"The food at camp won't last long, Seebaer," said Joannes out of the blue, trying to provoke a new conversation as they continued on their exploration.

"No. But time will be our reward."

"Certainly, and there's plenty of that to be had."

"If a ship doesn't pass our way soon, more time than we can bear will come our way."

"I was thinking," said Seebaer as a few more steps were taken, looking out upon the sea and in towards the land unknown to them both, "if these beetles and other insects we see all around us are edible."

Joannes screwed up his face for a second as he considered the idea of crunching into a beetle, pressing it between his teeth until its innards came rushing out of its arse and onto his tongue.

"I mean to say," continued Seebaer, "if the savages upon this land have learnt to survive, then why can't we?"

Joannes considered this for a moment.

"You might have something there, Seebaer. Yes indeed; struck a chord you have," congratulated Joannes in his round-about way, nodding his head in approval of the consideration. "And what better way to learn than from the savages themselves."

Seebaer stopped dead in his tracks, "What? You can't be serious?" said Seebaer.

"Why not?" said Joannes as his shoulders shrugged up and down. "They've lived on this land for as long as any ship came into view of the coast; even longer. They survive day to day. This is a strange land, an entirely new environment to what we are used to. The savages haven't attacked us."

"But we haven't come into any contact as yet," said Seebaer, not knowing of the sighting that Jan and Harmen had experienced. "What if they're hostile?"

"If they're hostile then we are dead already. The only way is to befriend them, search them out, share in their secrets in order to survive."

"Look, the sun is directly above us," indicated Seebaer. "What says we return with what news we have and then make suggestions."

"I honestly believe it's our only way. If a ship doesn't find us within the next few months then we will have to trust the savages of this land like the VOC trusts in those of Batavia and beyond." It was by these words that Seebaer seemed to be convinced.

They were both in agreement and turned on the spot, and commenced the trek back to where they had begun.

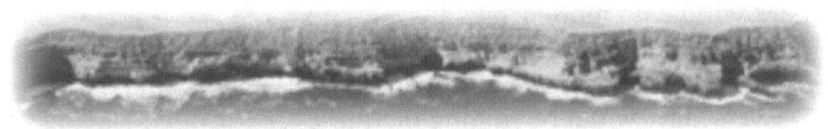

CHAPTER NINE

It was a little after midday when the survivors upon the cliff gave into their urges for something to eat. They gathered at the place which had been transformed into a temporary campsite, a small fire burning dull with embers cooled but still alive. Kindling was quickly added and the flames stirred into motion as a pot of water, filled from a nearby rock hole, was placed upon it, its base buried into the ash and charcoal. What meat remained was wrapped well and stored back in a barrel with a cover, before being placed in the shade, away from the flies.

Gerrit Jongbloet, one for the drinkers from nearer the cliff face, walked over and stood there next to those that were seated upon the earth.

"I've come to see if I can get something for the others to eat," said Gerrit, a shameful look of despair upon his face.

All of the others looked upon him and then to one another, before finally shifting their view to Ariaen.

"You'll have to wait, Gerrit," said Ariaen. "The sick must come first."

Hayman, the man with two broken legs, quickly voiced his opinion, "Give them nothing, I say; nothing at all."

"What is it to you, old man?" scolded Gerrit. "You'll be dead soon."

"Damn you to hell!" cursed Hayman.

"Enough!" and Ariaen was upon his feet in an instant. "You will have enough to eat," continued Ariaen, "but be warned; you and your friends must make amends and help with the work.

There will be no more drinks for any of you."

"Yes," said Gerrit. "Our supply is missing, only several bottles left from what we had secured aside... for a rainy day."

"Every day would be raining in your eyes," scoffed Hayman.

"Okay, so I was wrong, but I am hungry, too," defended Gerrit. "We are part of the crew, we deserve to get something to eat."

"Be warned, Gerrit, there are no other bottles left for you, every bottle found below has been opened and thrown into the sea. You must all help with what needs to be done or there will be nothing for you," said Ariaen. "And, Gerrit; we are more than you, it would be wise to help."

"Is that a threat, Ariaen?"

"Make of it what you will, but discipline must remain if we are to be successful in our plight."

"Very well," said Gerrit after a few seconds of silence. "I shall tell the others, but please give me some food so that I can go back with a full hand. The others... they are still very hungover. We can commence work in a few hours or more. Is this acceptable?"

"It is, Gerrit, but advise them first and then they can have some food. We're also going to have some rest, for the work is hard. The salvage is almost complete. A signal fire will be our next concern and the dead will have to be cremated... to stop the spread of disease."

"I understand," said Gerrit. "I'll go and tell the others and return shortly for some rations."

"Fine; you do that."

Gerrit turned and departed, leaving the main group to continue with their rest and cooking. A noise then came from beyond, a voice that sounded familiar.

"It's Jan," said Dirck. "I'd know his voice anywhere."

They all listened carefully and it came again, muffled by the background noise of the sea and the natural barrier of the thick scrub of tea-tree.

"Jan, over here," yelled Dirck.

"Help me. I need help," came the voice.

"Did he say 'help'?" asked Dirck of what he had heard.

"Yes," replied Pieter as he, too, stood. "Quickly, follow me."

Dirck and Pieter raced off through the scrub as fast as they dared, calling out every few seconds, closing the gap between themselves and Jan. When they finally fell upon him they saw that Harmen was upon his shoulder, draped over him like a rag doll, a dead weight with most of the colour drained from his face. Jan let the body fall as he fell to his knees and sobbed lightly.

"He was a good friend. There was nothing I could do," defended Jan.

"What happened?" asked Dirck.

"A snake bite," said Jan, and with the word came two looks of despair, for they had been completely void of thought on such dangers, but now more than ever, they needed to tread warily, wherever they went.

"Come, Jan, you aren't to blame for anything," comforted Dirck. "There's nothing that could be done."

"If only I had a knife, I could have cut his wound, sucked the poison from within him."

"It's finished now," said Dirck. "Come. We'll carry Harmen back to the fireplace. You take a rest. None of this is your fault."

"No," protested Jan. "I'll carry him, too. I was his friend, the best in the world."

"We'll all help," said Pieter.

CHAPTER TEN

"Help, come quickly," came the voice.

"What now?" said Wiebbe, looking up towards where the two men had moved.

"No, Wiebbe," said Willem, pointing towards the cliff. "Over there; it's Gerrit."

"Quickly, help," gasped Gerrit as he raced towards the fireplace.

"What's wrong, Gerrit?" asked Wiebbe, only slightly concerned, feeling as though an injustice had been served by Gerrit and the other three.

"Cornelius Brouwer has fallen off the cliff and down the slope. I think he hit his head. He isn't moving."

Wiebbe looked down to the three men in his care, "I can't leave these men. Quickly, take someone with you Gerrit... someone capable, not your friends; and see if he's hurt."

"I'll help," said Willem, standing up and preparing himself for duty.

"You stay there, Willem, and cook the food. We all need nourishment. Hendrik, you and Gerrit go and see what can be done."

"Aye," obeyed Hendrik without as much as a batter of the eyelids, grabbing Gerrit by the arm to help him upon his feet. The two men took off towards the scene of the accident.

Willem sat back down and stirred the meat and peas within the pot that he had under his control as Wiebbe looked down upon the open-eyed threesome, the wounded under his care.

"This is a fine mess, Willem. Two calls for help, three wounded... that's me and you, boy; that's it... just the two of us," Wiebbe turned to look at the boy. "I don't mind telling you that this very minute, right here and now, is the loneliest I have ever felt before in my entire life."

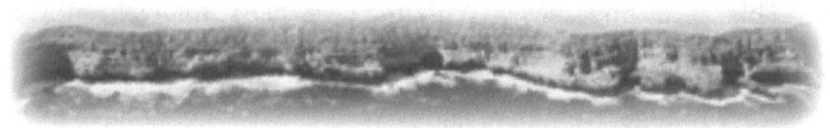

CHAPTER ELEVEN

Pieter, Dirck and Jan could be heard moving back through the scrub and no sooner did they fall upon the fireplace and Wiebbe was at their side ready to assist wherever he could.

They laid the body of Harmen upon the ground and in full sight of the three wounded, who in their state of misery could only contemplate their near future as being the same. Of the three that lay upon the ground with bandages and splints in place only one didn't consider himself as being familiar with Harmen, but he had come to know him during that first morning after the Zuytdorp had wrecked.

The body of Harmen was laid upon the ground and Wiebbe knelt down beside him, Dirk opposite and looking rather solemn, for Dirk knew that he was beyond saving.

"It's times like this that I wish we had a priest with us," said Wiebbe, "a man of comfort, a comforter of the sick."

"We had such a man," said Dirk.

"I know," replied Wiebbe.

"But he died in the wreck, during the storm."

Wiebbe looked Dirk in the eyes and understood his frustration too, for neither of them was a doctor but both had intelligence enough to understand the rudiments of providing aid to the sick. It comes naturally after many years at sea where men fall victim to scurvy and diseases of the tropics, where the shells of men fall victim of God's own vengeance... or so it would seem.

The split second silence was then pushed aside as Jan, standing there with something to say, opened his mouth and gave the news which all were dreading to hear.

"I saw a savage, a naked man with a spear and shield."

The others hanging around those injured and laying upon the ground, and even the breeze itself, stopped what was being done or talked about, to listen with great dread to what was to be said.

"I saw one of them, and Harmen saw him too," and after the incident with the snake he had come to change his mind on the circumstances of their arrival in hell. "He was dark and stood erect, holding his ground and eyeing us with hunger in his eyes. I could see and hear his mind in play, his wish to boil my flesh for eating, or to roast it above a fire. His thin shell showed how hungry he was, his eyebrows providing shelter to those dark eyes of his, the evil that they cast in our direction. If it wasn't for the fact that he was alone, he would have been after us."

"Was he all of that, Jan?" asked Pieter, still standing beside him.

"He was indeed, and much, much more," concluded Jan.

"Then we must prepare for the worst," said Ariaen. "Several knives have been salvaged."

"They'll do little against the thrust of a spear," said Dirk. "And what other weapons does he have: do 'they' have?"

"They're savages," reminded Wiebbe. "What can they have?"

"They have survived here, haven't they?" advised Pieter. "Lived upon this land, naked to the world, and survived the elements."

"And the damnation of God," said Marinus from his place upon the dirt, rubbing his palm across his broken ribs, the pain of speaking cast upon his face like the marks of a sculpture's chisel made upon rock.

"They're God's creatures too," said Willem, voicing his opinion.

"Savages like them don't have religion," said Jan. "I saw him both plain and simple, and saw his intentions. He was evil, very evil, and I wouldn't wish to confront a group of them for fear of death."

Gerrit and Hendrik then returned with bad news. Cornelius had died in the fall from the cliff, having hit his head hard upon a boulder before coming to an abrupt stop just half way down the slope of detritus.

"We dragged his body to where the others lay waiting," said Hendrik as he looked upon the form of Harmen. "What happened?"

"He was bitten by a snake and died," said Jan and all of those around quickly scanned the ground around them for their fear of snakes was as real as their fear of being stranded upon this land for the remainder of their miserable lives.

CHAPTER TWELVE

Before dusk had arrived upon the scene of the wreck and the survivors in the temporary campsite, Seebaer and Joannes had returned to their friends, smiles cast upon their faces, happy to be back after such a short time away. It was a miracle in itself, the safety they felt being amongst the group of other survivors, all of whom were in the same predicament and shared the same fears. It wasn't as if they'd be absent for any great length of time, or returning into the arms of a loved one. It was the comradeship that they needed, the comfort of another that shared the same will to live.

Both men listened intently to the story told, of how Cornelius had fallen to his death, how Harmen came to grief, of the savage seen beyond the scrub where the land was like a motionless sea of undulating plains, bare of life other than trees which sucked the land dry of all its moisture.

All of the survivors were now around the fire, a small yet necessary commodity, the centrepiece of their communion, two of the drunks, Jacob Albertsz and Jacobus Nuyts, still out cold, unconscious from there sucking on the last of the bottles of gin that had been hidden so well, five bottles between them which now lay smashed upon the ground, remnants of their poor discipline, empty bottles that only now could join the other bottles drained the night before. It was surprising that they were still alive. But it appeared that they had already been forgiven for blankets had been placed over them, to keep them warm as the cold of the night came rolling in from over the sea, where another cloudless night sucked the warmth from their very surroundings. How on earth did the savages survive such weather, walking around naked as they did?

Cornelis Lieffers then appeared from his work, his devotion to keeping busy, bringing another bucket with him filled with fresh water, water scooped by hand from a rock hole not far away.

"Cornelis, young friend," said Ariaen to the young man. "You work too hard and need to rest."

"I fear the thoughts that linger within me will surface and explode," said Cornelis, seemingly ashamed, willingly letting his guard down, his emotions betraying him, his exhaustion taking hold upon his very being.

"You need to rest, nevertheless," continued Ariaen. "There have been too many deaths already, and I don't wish to see another." Ariaen looked at the man still coming of age. "Will you sit and join us? Seebaer and Joannes have returned with news."

"Is it good news?" asked Cornelis.

"We've found somewhere that will accept a rescue boat, just to the south," offered Seebaer.

"But not to sail one?"

"We don't think so, Cornelis, no," said Seebaer with a downturned eye. "But we intend to go to the north, to search for another place from which to launch a boat. The work you've achieved alone will provide us with enough wood for a small boat; I'm sure of it."

"Yes," said Cornelis, his heart lifted. "Enough to make two boats. All we need to do is drag the wood from the platform and up the embankment."

"Yes, indeed," said Ariaen. "We'll do just that tomorrow morning. But we want you to go with Seebaer and Joannes tomorrow, to support them."

"They'd be faster with two," said Cornelis. "Wouldn't they?

And what of the work here?"

"We are plenty," added Ariaen. Gerrit, Jacob and Jacobus will be joining us tomorrow; to be put to work... isn't that right, Gerrit?"

"Yes," said Gerrit, looking up into the eyes of Cornelis. "The other two will have sore heads but with a little food and water they will do just fine."

Cornelis smiled and nodded, "Okay, I'll go."

"Great," said Ariaen. "Now sit down and have something to eat; rest those weary bones of yours, for tomorrow you will journey far."

"It's just a day trip, isn't it?" asked Cornelis.

"You didn't hear?" prompted Pieter.

"Hear?"

"Of Jan and the savage?" said Gerrit.

"No," said Cornelis. "What savage?" and the ordeal with the remnants of the land were provided to Cornelis to the very last detail.

"So you see, we need at least three, and armed with weapons, too," said Ariaen.

Cornelis nodded acceptance for the last thing he wished to do was let down the other men. Willem thought how proud he would be to take after Cornelis, to be willing to do whatever it takes to survive, to relish any task handed down, to devote himself to any given opportunity.

"And I think we should stop thinking of them as savages," said Joannes. "If a ship fails to be drawn to our presence then they might be the only way to survive, the only avenue open to us. They are natives, not savages."

"Only time will tell, Joannes," said Ariaen. "For the time being we need to explore towards the north where much coastline is known to exist. Many ships have used the coast to mark their progress, almost three hundred miles of it... if my calculations are correct."

"And I'll go too," said Jan. He looked at the others. "I can't stay here, not with my friend having departed from this world."

"We'll be saying our goodbyes soon enough, Jan," said Ariaen. "Don't you want to stay and say farewell?"

"I have said my farewell, carrying him upon my back for many hours in the heat of the day. I sometimes wish that winter was here already," and he kicked at the dirt.

"It's upon us, just not as severe as we're used to," said Ariaen, scratching at the bandage covering the gash in his head and looking out over the sea towards the west. "It has just begun."

"If it wasn't for the heat, that snake might not even exist."

"There is much we don't know about this land. Everything needs to be learnt. The ways of one snake isn't necessarily the same as another. Take that creature, for example, the one you say was jumping in great bounds across the ground... that in itself is unbelievable. How can such a thing exist?"

"But it does," said Jan.

"And we believe you," confirmed Ariaen. "If you wish to go north then go, we won't stop you," and to change the subject he looked to Willem. "How's the meat and peas?"

"Ready," said Willem.

It seemed that death was all around them and that it couldn't be avoided. It was one mishap after the next. Some drew on the situation as a condemned ending to a sadly shortened existence whilst others looked upon it as an opportunity to shake the defeat from within them and to pour on the courage to continue as best they could, moulding a new life for themselves upon a land that they simply did not know. They would do as Joannes and Seebaer had suggested and try to make friends with the natives, people of the land, no longer savages of the mind.

The bounds of survival were commencing to surface and for those with the courage to take it all into an open palm... for them the future was ready to be written.

Of the man that had fallen from the edge of the cliff; he had fallen to his death and was left there at the bottom, simply dragged over to the pile of dead that currently existed on the shoreline platform. The mass of flesh was beyond them all, hard to fathom such wasted life, the deaths of both young and old, those of command and structure, seamen, women, and boys that had enlisted to do a man's job at sea. Of the little children, only one was found and placed at the pile as it grew in size, the others had been lost by way of the sea, the waves taking the fragile forms of human remains to a burial site which would never be discovered.

That evening there was much to reflect upon and reflect they did, but mostly in silence. They were all too tired to do much about anything; so they lay there, asleep, half asleep, or simply contemplating the future, but rest was the order of the night and so rest was quickly secured by all, whether it be a little slumber or a lot, and every single one of them was appreciative of the meat and the peas, stomachs silent for the night.

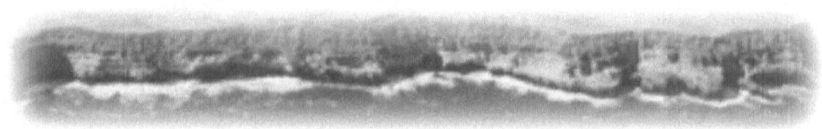

CHAPTER THIRTEEN

7th June.

The drunken men were now sober and their heads completely clear by the following morning's first light, to see the errors of their ways, but not to admit them, and along with the sunlight came a fresh wind from the west, a steadily increasing wind which dragged along with it a mass of cloud. With broken bottles left to remain as a memorial to those that had perished at this site, the shards and pieces reflected light, there in the rays of the sun, to just sit there undisturbed, unmoving, to be clambered upon by ants, to remain mostly undisturbed for the future, a future which had not yet been set for those that remained. And of all the futures that would greet the drunkards as they woke from the misery that they had created for themselves, was another body, a body now relinquished of his ghostly spirit, for Francisco Roelofsz, the man with the broken leg and punctured gut, had died. But of all the things that mattered most was the fact that they had now all come together, to be as one community.

And the damn flies, they were nothing less than a plague, not to mention the growing concern over the ants that clambered over the sick without remorse.

Hayman Jorisz pulled his fingers from his bandage and placed them beneath his nose, withdrawing them quickly for the smell upon his fingers was disgusting, the most horrid thing he'd ever smelt in his life before. It smelt of decayed meat, of death. He was gangrenous. He looked over to the others, Seebaer, Joannes, Cornelis and Jan having departed already for the north.

With an upturned nose he was about to request help; some water in which to wash his fingers when he heard two men approaching; Jacob and Jacobus. Hayman simply watched them in silence, his hatred for them written upon his face. He knew deep inside of him that his legs would have to be amputated, cut off from above the knee. What was there to help him with the pain, the torture of having himself mutilated? There was no gin... it was gone, every drop, wasted upon drunkards who weren't strong enough to handle the horrors of the shipwreck that had seen them cast upon this land like the forgotten choruses of an unfamiliar song heard but once, drained from the head, like the waters of a river so hastily spilled into the sea. He would have to show that he was man enough to accept the disfigurement, to hold back his cries of pain, to show that he was a man of men and as strong as any of them that had survived.

And the two men walked past him, glancing down but briefly as they took several more steps towards the congregation, Willem, Pieter, Ariaen, Hendrik, Dirck, Wiebbe and Gerrit, not to mention the two soon-to-be-dead.

"Sit down," said Ariaen in invitation. "Have something to eat. There isn't much but we are hoping to secure food later on today; some shellfish and maybe other supplies."

"Thank you," said Jacob as he sat and pulled a slightly curved piece of bark into his chest, a little meat and peas sitting there upon the piece of bark, several ants already having a go at the meagre pickings, waiting for him to shovel the meal down his gullet.

"And for you, too, Jacobus."

"Thank you."

Gerrit looked upon his so-called friends, those that had successfully corrupted him into accepting the gin, "How do you both feel?"

"I'm fine," said Jacob.

"Me too," said Jacobus with a mouthful of food.

"And why wouldn't you be, you scum!" cursed Hayman, thinking of the pain to be endured. "You take all the gin and scoff it down, and now you come here, not having done a single days work other than a few minutes, from what I hear, and now you partake of our sustenance as though you have worked hard since our shipwreck here upon this horrid place."

"It's for all of us," said Ariaen, indicating the little food they had, but understanding the hate, but not the inability to forgive. "Let's hear no more of it."

"It's easy for you to say," said Hayman, a tear slowly filling his eye before drying in the breeze that blew in from beyond the sea and across the land. "I'm to be amputated and there is no gin left; no wine; no beer; no medicine."

Gerrit stirred and spoke softly to the man in anguish, "I have a bottle, saved for you."

The two drunks shot a glance apiece at Gerrit.

"Where is it," stabbed Jacob.

"Enough! You swine! Damn you to hell!"

"Sit still, Hayman," ordered Wiebbe as he raced over to the man as he tried in vain to claw his way to Jacob, to kill him.

"You have sinned," said Gerrit, stabbing a glance of pure hatred at Jacob.

"And so have you," answered Jacobus for his off-sider.

"Gerrit is one of us," spoke Ariaen. "You two men have been given food and water, and this is how you repay your debt, by illustrating a growing need for gin, to satisfy your weakness."

Jacob held out his hand for all to see, shaking out of control, unable to stop the tremors from within.

"I'm not a doctor; you can't be helped," said Ariaen. "You helped yourself to the gin, now help yourself to overcome your wicked desire."

"I can't," said Jacob in all sincerity and regret, a look of terror upon his face as the juice from the peas and meat dribbled from the corners of his mouth and down his chin. "I must have it; please. There was plenty on the Zuytdorp before she was wrecked and my desire is still strong."

"There are others in need of it more than you," said Wiebbe as he leant forward and smelt the wound, sorrow filling his face as he stroked with great compassion the forehead of Hayman.

"Pieter; Dirck... will you help me?"

"What is it, Wiebbe?" asked Dirck.

"It's time," answered Wiebbe with a plain face, undefined and solemn. "Time to take these legs off; the sooner the better."

The sorrow within Hayman's eyes was like the look of an innocent child, a hideous crime about to be committed; the look upon Jacobs was similar, but filled with deceit.

Silence... the men moved to the task in silence, forgetting their food and water, forgetting their comfort, thinking only of the poor man about to be operated upon.

They moved Hayman, sobbing, away from the others, towards the south where the screams would not be heard; Ariaen went too. Embers were carried by Willem, for he had been asked to help raise a small fire, a fire which was to be employed in preparing the cutting tool – a knife. It was large enough to be handled as a cutting device and could be used to chop, to chop through the bone.

Willem returned to get some cloth, some rope, and a little extra kindling for the fire, several small logs not going astray, and as he returned he passed Gerrit who stepped off to retrieve the hidden bottle of gin, and behind him, close enough to see but far enough so not to be heard, followed Jacob. Willem ignored what he saw, not thinking anything of it, focussing only upon his task and his task alone, to try and take his mind away from what was about to happen: all he needed to do was to ready the fire and bandages.

CHAPTER FOURTEEN

Gerrit stepped out amidst the broken bottles and saw the place where he had hidden the last of the gin, behind a small tea-tree and beneath a large rock, where a hidden lair had been scraped from beneath it.

He got down upon his knees and commenced to excavate the pain-killer when a noise caught his ear. He turned his head and saw Jacob standing over him, and Jacob's face screwed up tight as he brought a large rock down upon the man's head, killing him instantly, grabbing for the bottle which had been revealed, the neck sticking out like a sore thumb, the best sight Jacob had seen in his entire life.

He wasted no time at all and soon had it open, swallowing in great gulps all that he could fit into his mouth. Before long it was empty, as though it was nothing but a flagon of water, drained of every last drop.

Jacob suddenly turned and saw Jacobus standing there, having followed soon after, seeing that Jacob was up to no good.

"You bastard," scolded Jacobus. "What have you done?"

Jacob looked down at the deceased Gerrit, but Jacobus was referring to the gin, not the deceased.

"It's gone, every damn drop. You took it for yourself," said Jacobus before the reality of the situation hit him hard. "You've killed Gerrit, killed him for a bottle of gin; the last to be had. My God, what have you done?"

"I had to... I..." stammered Jacob, seemingly drunk already from what he had administered to himself.

CHAPTER FIFTEEN

Back at the fireplace, where Willem had returned to secure more bandages, Hendrik looked to the boy for confirmation on something he'd heard in the distance.

"Did you hear that, Willem?"

Willem stared off into the distance and then back to Hendrik, realising full well what it was.

"It's Jacob, and Jacobus; they've gone after Gerrit."

Hendrik looked down upon the sleeping form of Marinus, out cold and oblivious to what was going on, having been awake and in pain for most of the night.

"Stay here, Willem, I'm going to see what's going on."

"Here," urged Willem, thinking straight from the top of his head, "take this," and handed the knife to him before moving towards where Wiebbe and the others were waiting.

Hendrik took the knife without second thought and raced towards the commotion, upon the scene in what seemed to be a moment's notice, to see Jacob and Jacobus fighting, rolling around upon the ground, Gerrit unmoving where he laid, blood running freely from the wound upon the top of his head.

"What have you done?" Hendrik said in disbelief of the struggle between the two men, and Jacobus fell from the ledge, clawing at the earth as he slipped and fell, the short fall upon rocks below seeing to his own demise.

Jacob turned, his eyes blazed over by the gin, his mouth in a snarl, all manner of civilization gone from his face. He was no longer a man but the devil possessed and with the bloodied rock still in his hand he circled Hendrik, motioning him to fight, trying to corner him closer to the edge of the cliff.

"I have a knife, Jacob," advised Hendrik. "You don't stand a chance. Put the rock down, forget all of this. We're here to help, all of us; I am... here. Let me help you."

"I curse you... damned, bloody fool. I got more than you," stammered Jacob and held up his hand, high above his head, rock clenched in his fist. "I have the rock." He looked back down into Hendrik's eyes and raced towards him, the rock in motion, an extension of Jacob's arm, a weapon with which he was prepared to kill, but he stumbled and Hendrik stepped aside, Jacob falling to his death, too.

Hendrik just stood there, disbelief within him, his mind unable to calculate what the hell was going on. This was not how man was supposed to survive. What manner of evil could possess another to commit such heinous crimes against his fellow man? It then suddenly dawned upon him that he too had plenty to repent, for his vicious treatment of others before now was not to be forgotten. He had tried to become leader, to have the ability to sway judgement over those under his command, but now... he didn't want it. He was glad that Ariaen had received more votes than he, he was happy to have lost to a better man, for Ariaen was proving, day in and day out, that he was a good man with a clear vision for the future. It's what was needed, a strong man to lead a volatile group, a bunch of men who would have trouble finding their way in this new world, where the devil played with the souls of those unfortunate enough to be cast upon a land with little water and seemingly nothing to eat.

Hendrik could only whimper to himself, feelings of sorrow filling him like a carafe filled with water. He would have to come to grips with it all or come undone at the seams. He had but little choice.

CHAPTER SIXTEEN

By the time Hendrik had returned to where Pieter, Dirck and Wiebbe were readied for amputation, Willem tending the fire and checked over the supplies he had placed neatly beside Wiebbe, Ariaen sat silently at Hayman's head, ready to assist where possible, ready to obey orders as they were given to him.

"Willem," said Wiebbe, "Thank you, but it's time for you to go back to the main fire."

"But I can help—."

"No, you have done enough," concurred Pieter as he smiled at the boy. "Go and get yourself something more to eat, or better still, prepare something for all of us, for we'll be hungry after the job is done."

Willem nodded acceptance of the task and turned to depart, bumping into Hendrik as he stepped away, forgetful of Hendrik's intervention upon the two drunk men. No sooner was he out of earshot and the others asked Hendrik what had happened, swayed more by the look upon the man's face.

"They're dead," said Hendrik in a half daze, not quite believing the words as they stumbled from his mouth.

"Dead?" repeated Dirck.

"All three," nodded Hendrik.

Pieter stood, "Maybe you're wrong, maybe we should have another look."

A hand lashed out and grabbed at Pieter's leg; it was Hayman.

"The bastards deserved to die," said Hayman

"No one deserves to die in this place," said Pieter, looking down upon the man to be operated on, "no matter what their faults."

"They are dead," repeated Hendrik. "I saw two fall to their death and Gerrit has a wound to his head, a deathblow severe enough to kill him outright."

"Where's his body?" asked Pieter.

"At the cliff where he was killed."

"No, Pieter," said Dirck. "Don't go now, leave him. He's dead," Dirck looked at Hendrik, "there's nothing that can be done. Our task now is to help Hayman."

"You're right," said Pieter as he took his position beside the man to prepare for the task of holding the man down.

And that was the last of the words for a while as Hayman's legs were unbandage, the smell of defeat hitting them all, the mass of swelling revealed to them all, the discolouration taking full effect upon their hidden emotions, and the wound where the bone had, not so long ago, broken the skin and was open to the air.

Wiebbe was to do the cutting, and Dirck and Pieter were to hold Hayman's arms and upper body as motionless as possible, Dirck next to Wiebbe so that he could take over the task of hacking through the bone if the need arose. Hendrik sat at the ready at Hayman's feet, feet that were soon to be separated from the whole.

"No, Hendrik," said Dirck, cautioning the man to the requirement. "Get beside Pieter and help with restricting the upper leg... the thigh; keep it still.

'It'... a part of the body, not of Hayman, referred to an object, not of flesh. Hayman noted the course of words and the procedure to be conducted, Wiebbe's manner of expression. Wiebbe had already separated the task and his friend, the body to his front no more familiar to him than a sack of potatoes, for the way in which he was to deliver this man's pain was beyond contemplation, beyond belief. The last thing Wiebbe wished to do was to think of Hayman, as Hayman. No distraction was needed in this, Hayman's time of need. No manner of yelling or screaming, no amount of struggling or demand, nothing at all would stop Wiebbe in his tracks as he operated upon the legs to be removed. Once started it could not be stopped. It must be done in the shortest amount of time.

Willem was sitting beside the fire, cooking as he sat, thinking about what was to unfold not so far through the scrub. His only wish was for Hayman to survive the surgery; but that soon changed. Once the screaming started, the thick piece of leather between Hayman's jaws having served little of its purpose, Willem could only wish for silence to reign around him. It was shear torture, the sounds of pain and torment, the screams coming in unbroken cycle, filling the air with horror. Tears then welled up within Willem's eyes, the noise too much to bear, and he rolled over on his side, rolled up in a tiny ball, clutching his palms tightly upon his ears, and still the screams came reverberating through him as though the devil himself was standing beside him and holding back the cushion of his palms against his ears. There was nothing that could compare with those fifteen long minutes, the screams finally coming to an end.

Willem removed his palms from his ears, thankful that it was over, praising the Lord that he had stopped the torment, thanking God for answering his prayers, for bringing him silence. He wiped his eyes and sat back up.

It was only minutes later that Pieter appeared at the fire and stopped as he stepped next to the hearth, a look of solemnity about him.

"What is it?" asked Willem, thinking he knew the answer but afraid to say it out loud.

"Hayman is dead," answered Pieter. "The pain was too much for him."

And Willem began to cry once more for it was his fault. It was he, Willem, that had requested an end to the screaming; it was his prayers to God, for him to put an end to the torturous noise; yes indeed, it was he, Willem, that had asked for Hayman's death to be delivered this day. And his prayers were answered.

"What? What was that?" came a tired voice as Marinus awoke from his slumber, having missed all that had happened. "Who's dead?"

The wind commenced to pick up a little, blowing fiercer now than it had some twenty minutes before, Pieter's words a little muffled by the growing ferocity of the storm as it made its way in from the coast.

CHAPTER SEVENTEEN

Seebaer, Joannes, Cornelis and Jan were making seemingly good progress as they continued towards the north when their attention had been diverted to the growing tension within them all.

The basic lay of the land was similar as it was to the south and also the west; though the further west one proceeded the more there was for the eye to see... an almost barren wasteland of semi-desert, a rainfall average of just eight inches per year being cast upon the land.

It was most inhospitable, from the limestone cliffs and in towards undulating and featureless sandplains of virtual monotony where thickets of acacia and banksia could be found, the bush acting like little islands of shade from the sun where birds could park and enjoy the tranquillity of their surrounds. As for the margin between this barren landscape and the limestone cliffs, it was little more than a boundary of coastal dunes of chalky earth covered in salt-tolerant coastal heath and acacia scrub.

The limestone platform continued along the coast, as it was near the shipwreck of the Zuytdorp, the size of the platform ranging in width, rolling in similar contrast to the waves forming a wavering line upon any beach.

There appeared to be no permanent water source in the area, from what the men could see, but the aboriginals knew where the rock holes and soaks were, wells of life-sustaining water, the liquid gold needed in order to preserve life, but such soaks were almost five miles away and not on the coastal fringe.

The approaching storm had been building up over the past several hours and it wasn't long before they decided upon taking some form of action against the foul weather which would undoubtedly fall upon them.

"We'll have to make shelter, soon," said Joannes to the others. "This storm isn't going to relent nor pass-us-by."

"I agree,' said Cornelis, shifting the blanket upon his shoulder, it being tied with a single strand of rope with a loop, it being slung up and over his left arm.

"Where to, that's the question," stated Seebaer. "This cloth we have with us isn't going to do much against this wind, and the blankets we have are going to be useless unless we can find shelter."

"How far do you think we've come?" asked Jan.

"Why? Do you want to turn back already," said a joking Cornelis, unafraid of a little bad weather and hard work.

Jan was seen to take the comment the wrong way, interpreting it as an insult, "You think I'm scared; lazy perhaps?"

"No," winced Cornelis. "I was simply commenting... look, it doesn't matter. I too would prefer to accept any option; but even at the camp, there's little to no shelter."

"You're right," accepted Jan, "I'm, sorry."

"Well, we need to find somewhere," said Seebaer, "and the sooner, the better."

"We've come about ten miles is my guess," answered Cornelis, a quick calculation of time and pace being considered. "But it's so hard to tell when there isn't any sun by which to tell the time."

"My feet are as sore as hell," said Seebaer.

"Mine too," added Jan.

"Courtesy of the shipwreck and these damn conditions," concluded Cornelis for them all. "Let's try heading inland," he said to Seebaer. "There will be trees there, will there not?"

"Yes," answered Seebaer with little emotion, hunched over and shielding his face with an open palm as the heavens opened up and the downpour commenced, an opening to a storm which would rage for many hours, the suddenness of the downpour precipitated by a lightning strike that shook the earth they were standing upon.

"Come, let's go; quickly," voiced Cornelis as he led the way into the unknown.

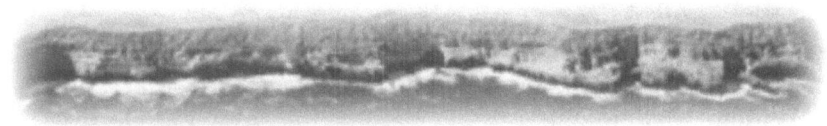

CHAPTER EIGHTEEN

The rain fell in buckets, the gullies filling up temporarily as they led the water away from the undulating ground of the open sandplains and into the sea, small torrents of water falling over the cliff of limestone.

Willem was hunched over and seemed very pale, the shelter they had struck providing sufficient shelter from the pouring rain but not from the penetrating cold. The boy was shaking like a leaf and he looked like hell, sweat started to fall from him freely.

All of the men had managed to gather together, endeavouring with all their ability to harness the body heat as a tool of survival; only Dirck and Marinus remained apart, just several feet away and laying beside each other, a large rock pile at their head where red hot embers from the fire had been placed in an effort to keep them from being completely doused by the rain, a similar construction amidst the others who now looked upon Willem with concern.

The symptoms had come out from nowhere, one minute he seemed fine and the next he seemed to be suffering.

Wiebbe held his palm against the boy's head and shook his head, "He has a fever, but from what I don't know."

"This damn land and the savages upon it," said Hendrik, obviously concerned for his own health as he pushed away to the farthest corner of their small shelter, the sail above his head leaking slightly, several drops of rain penetrating the fabric and falling upon him. He wrapped the blanket he held tightly around him.

"No," said Ariaen. "I don't believe that. No one else is suffering."

"So he's the first," said Hendrik, "that's all; the first to suffer."

Willem was clutching rather hard at his stomach. He was in much pain and seemingly a little delusional, looking here and there, but not at anything in particular. It was then that he vomited all he'd eaten that day, the meat, the peas, and the little shellfish he'd managed to consume.

"Poisoned by his own hand," said Hendrik. "Greed it is, that's the answer; his greed has seen to this torment being delivered. God knows when one is being greedy."

"It has nothing to do with poison," said Pieter, holding onto the boy's arm in an effort to offer some comfort.

"Too much food, you fool," said Hendrik sarcastically.

"I know what you mean, Hendrik," spat Pieter out of character, "but the boy has had nothing more or less than any of us. We have all had the same."

"Did anyone notice anything strange?" asked Wiebbe of the others. All shook their heads. "Dirck; Marinus; did you notice anything wrong with the boy?"

"What?" came Dirck's reply, he in a daydream, contemplating his death from where he lay farthest away, seeing with sudden surety that Willem was in further difficulty, clutching at his stomach. "What's that? What else is wrong with Willem?"

"You tell me," answered Wiebbe. "Did you see anything wrong with the boy earlier on?"

"Not, not a thing," said Dirck. "What are his symptoms?"

"He's vomiting, has a fever and is in a lot of pain."

"Maybe it's something he ate," came the reply from Dirck.

A smirk fell upon Hendrik as he looked Pieter and Ariaen in the eye, "Told you, didn't I?"

Wiebbe tried to gain Willem's attention, lifting his head and staring directly into him, finding nothing but clear vision and nil response.

"Willem; do you hear me?" asked Wiebbe.

"Of course he hears——."

"Shut up, Hendrik," and the death stare from Wiebbe shut Hendrik's mouth for the remainder of their discomfort, sitting there beneath the shelter so hastily made. "Willem, look into my eyes. Do you hear me?"

"Nothing," said Pieter. "Let's put him down and make him as comfortable as possible, explore this later."

"There may not be a later," confided Wiebbe. "Whatever it is that Willem is suffering might very well be the end of him."

"It might very well be the end of all of us," added Ariaen.

"I pray not," concluded Pieter.

CHAPTER NINETEEN

8th June.

Later in the night, when the stars came out to greet life on earth, the clouds having passed and the waters of the storm having drained away via gully and simply having been swallowed up by the dry land, invisible creatures could be heard giving their songs freely for all to hear. There was pleasantness about the sounds that stretched out through the night, over the folds in the ground, mating calls amongst them, disparate to anything the men of the Zuytdorp had heard before.

Dirck and Marinus were asleep on the far side of the hearth, Ariaen and Pieter fast asleep, as was Willem, seemingly over his spout of misfortune. Wiebbe, on the other hand, was wide awake and listening to the sounds all around him, trying to decipher what he could of the beatles, grubs, insects and nocturnal animals, species he'd never known existed, let alone seen with his own eyes.

It seemed to him that the boy, Willem, had recovered sufficiently to be left unattended, a little colour having returned to his cheeks, his pulse seemingly normal, the fever gone and no sweat to speak of being present; the boy was even sleeping comfortably and with his arms loose across his body... no longer was he crunched up in a ball and holding for dear life to his stomach. Whatever was wrong with the lad had been put right... he was out of danger.

Wiebbe wasn't an educated man, but neither was he stupid.

He'd learnt a little of medicine and of comforting the sick and could tell rather well the time of night by looking to the heavens above. It was in this way that he could see that the morning would be upon them in three to four hours, the storm having passed them by without too much of a problem being encountered.

He stood up and stepped from the shelter and headed towards the higher ground, through some thick scrub and following his intuition, some scratching noises coming from not too far away.

He'd gone several hundred feet when he came across what he considered might have been the proposed campsite suggested by Jan earlier on, for the ocean could be seen quite clearly from it. He continued on his way. Within minutes he fell upon a little bare ground, a good site for a camp although only a little more rewarding when compared to the other, except for the fact that it would serve well as a makeshift camp for any sick. Many thoughts then travelled his mind, on life and death, disease and cure, medicine, food and water. The scratching noise had been forgotten and he continued to wander around as he made his way back to the campsite and bedded down once more, unable to sleep with his mind full of theory and consideration.

CHAPTER TWENTY

The early morning had brought Ariaen and Pieter to the fire, Wiebbe stoking it with a stick, getting it ready for a breakfast of peas and shellfish, the meat, what was left of it, to be saved for later on.

"Have you been up long?" asked Pieter of Wiebbe as he and Ariaen sat down upon the ground, a little damp but not overly uncomfortable.

"Not long," answered Wiebbe. "I couldn't sleep and so went for a walk and thought to get the fire started. We don't have much dry wood left."

"There should be plenty," remarked Adriane. "Enough for several days, at least until we can gather more."

"I was thinking," said Wiebbe, "we might need to make another campsite, further away from where we are."

"What in God's name, for?" queried Ariaen.

"The edge of the cliff is a dangerous place, in particular if Willem is to fall into another dream-state. We also have to consider the added discomfort of the spray from the ocean during unsavoury storms."

"But that's not the only reason, is it?" added Pieter. "I see the look in your eye, Wiebbe."

Wiebbe couldn't put it any other way, none other than to come clean with his idea, "I've had a look further inland, towards where Jan and Harmen ventured the other day. I came across a great spot which offered a little protection from the wet and the rise in elevation was enough to see the ocean. It would be rather easy to maintain a watch from the comfort of a warm fire and we could make it ready with a signal fire as proposed earlier."

"And?" prodded Pieter.

"We could make another campsite just beyond that where the sick could be placed; like a hospital."

"You're concerned over Willem, aren't you?" asked Ariaen.

"Not just him. Look at Marinus. He seems well enough, but what if he turns gangrenous... should we have to suffer the smell?"

"Look," began Pieter, "I have no objection, but if we're going to have more than one camp then I think I should be with the sick, and remain permanently by their side."

"With Willem?" said Wiebbe.

"Yes, that's right."

"I see no problem with that," nodded Wiebbe. "Dirck and I will have to take turns in looking after any sick, regardless, and your assistance is no less appreciated. It's a duty which must be performed. But there is one other thing which I'm concerned about."

"And that is?" asked Ariaen, waving the flies away from his face.

"A lookout near where the sandplains begin. Just one thousand feet from the sandplains there's an old camp; Jan told me of it... told all of us."

"Where Harmen was bitten by that snake," said Pieter as he turned his face away, upset by the death of one of them.

"Yes, that's right. We can maintain a vigil on the natives, see what they do, and act as an early warning for the others if they should approach. It already has a large tree nearby for preparing food... hanging a dead carcass... and there's a large rock there, seemingly used for grinding corn or other substances. There must be food nearby, something we don't know about as yet. We must explore all options and keep our eyes open. Staying in one spot just won't do. We need to commence with the laying of traps for food; and we don't want a dead carcass attracting any wild animals."

"There aren't enough of us for three sites, Wiebbe," consoled Ariaen. "You've already condemned—."

"That's rather a strong word," protested Wiebbe.

"Nevertheless, you suggest placing the sick plus another, either yourself or Dirck, in a camp for the sick; that accounts for three of us, not to mention Pieter. That leaves seven others, including me."

"We would only need to place two men at a time near the sandplains; the others could maintain the camp nearest the sea, watching for a passing ship."

"I think he's right," agreed Pieter. "It's against my better judgement to separate Willem from the remainder, but I see the logic."

Ariaen was silent for a few seconds and then nodded acceptance, "Very well. We'll tell the others when they wake and commence immediately."

"There is one other thing," said Wiebbe. "We must burn the dead where they lay and as soon as possible, ensuring they burn. I don't see the point in dragging this out too much longer. We'll do what we can with the dead stacked near the cliff; place enough deadfall upon them so as to incinerate them all. It's the only way."

The others nodded in silent agreement for they all knew deep down that Wiebbe was right. They could not afford an epidemic, a flood of disease spreading through what remained of the precious cargo of flesh and bone... them. Their lives meant more to them than anything else and they were all sure in their minds that the dead would forgive their grievances against them.

CHAPTER TWENTY-ONE

Seebaer and his companions fared reasonably well in the conditions that had fallen upon them, considering that all they had was a little sailing cloth and several small blankets. The tinderbox they had carried with them was of little use as there was no dry material for which to start a fire at the time when they needed it the most. As for the food, that was all gone, their stomachs filled prior to departing the shipwreck and filling up again during the storm.

They were thankful that it hadn't lasted as long as they dread but now weighed up the options open to them.

In most places the cliff proved to be impassable and so the gathering of shellfish would be a major problem for them, and no other means of support availed itself, including the sighting of a rock hole from which to top up the only water-carrying device they had: an old pot with a loose piece of cloth as a lid.

Without fire, food, or water, they were already in dire straits.

The misery of the men wasn't so contagious, for all were suffering the same, but misery of such weight won't allow a man to continue on a journey that offered little reward.

Huddled around the old pot, now replenished due to the night's rain, and blankets draped around them, they considered the only option open.

"We have to return immediately," stated Seebaer without argument being voiced, only nods of the head being received.

"I think we can all agree to that," said Jan. "It's against my better judgement, but only as I volunteered for the task; but what choice do we have? Shall we start now?"

Seebaer nodded, "I'll lead the way if you wish and..." the sudden fall of silence attracted all eyes, ears intent on being the first to find out what it was that had drawn Seebaer's attention.

"What is it?" asked Joannes in a whisper.

Seebaer held his finger to his mouth and then the noise came again. There was something moving towards them, something close to the ground and seemingly dragging something along. It was a rustling noise of slow approach, the crunching and debris beneath a heavy weight.

Seebaer stood up, half crouched, and as he looked out in the direction his eyes popped out of his head and he sat again.

The others looked upon him in terror, afraid for what it might be, a savage, or a group of them, something heinous; who knew what this land held in secret ready to be unleashed against them.

"Seebaer, what is it?" Joannes asked again.

"A large creature with very small legs; it's almost as big as Willem," answered Seebaer as he placed his finger against his lip one more time.

"Listen to me carefully and trust in what I say," said Seebaer. "Do you trust me?"

Everyone nodded, yes.

"When I say go you must all stand and take up a stick or rock; kick with your foot if you must... throw a blanket upon it, all of you. Do what you can. He will be slow because his legs are small." Seebaer looked around once more and nodded, "Are you ready... now!"

And the four men rushed to their feet, three of which didn't know what they were up against.

Before them was a wombat, large and plump, a great mass of flesh ready to be made into stew.

Blankets were thrust upon the creature, stones taken from the ground and thrown, a large rock was then lifted by Cornelis and he delivered a shocking blow to the creature's neck as it moved, a blanket falling from it. It moved with great speed away from them as other blankets were thrown and then picked up, and the chase was on. The commotion of the hunt was in full swing, all in complete disbelief at something that looked like nothing they'd seen before, although Joannes had seen a picture of a badger once, a creature from England that looked remarkably similar: as far as he could tell.

Colourful language filled the air as orders flew from one to the other, the mass of energy now exerted by all four men beyond what they thought was within them, the adrenalin rush for fresh meat overwhelming them all.

The wombat was under great stress now, several blankets thrown upon him not budging, getting caught around him as he tried to step away from the vicious men that now surrounded him.

The men closed in on the creature and lashed out, several beats to the head connecting well and it was then that Seebaer fell upon it with the only knife that was carried between them all, penetrating the back of the animal. He withdrew it then and stabbed again, and again, and again; and before they knew it the creature was dead, and with the deed complete the animal was skewered from mouth to anus with one of the poles employed to hold up the sail cloth during inclement weather, sharpened at one end and pushed through with a great amount of effort.

The pole was carried between two of them as the group made their way back towards camp, exchanging positions from time to time, taking rest breaks as they grew more hungry and tired.

It was very tempting to bring their return to a momentary halt, in order for the four men to cut away a small portion of the beast they had captured, to cook it up and eat it fresh. They could already savour the fat of the meat, imagine it running down their faces, spoiling the rags on their backs that they called clothes.

But the time they needed to find dry wood and then bring a fire to life was beyond their contemplations.

The trek back would have been considered as the most tiring, where the men were exhausted and without proper nourishment, but the fact that they had caught food for the first time gave them such an amazing uplift in spirits that they almost found themselves singing, and if it wasn't for a lack in energy they may very well have broken out into song.

And as the morning grew into early afternoon, Seebaer looked up and saw something to his front, something that gained his immediate attention, for he saw smoke.

"Do you see that?" shouted Seebaer for the rest to look, his arm pointing in the direction of where their camp was situated.

"A signal fire!" presumed Jan, breaking out into a run in order to see for himself the white sails of a ship coming towards the cliff - but there was none.

"Don't; Jan," yelled Seebaer. "No ship is expected until at least the eleventh of June... today's the eighth."

"Leave him, Seebaer," said Joannes. "Let him run. He'll find out soon enough."

"But maybe it is a ship," said Cornelis.

"No, Seebaer is right."

"Then what is it?" asked Cornelis.

Seebaer stopped in his tracks and turned to look at the pole bearers, "It must be the dead. They're torching the bodies, burning their decay, cleansing the air we breathe."

"So be it," added Joannes. "All the less work for us. It'll make a good fire for this prize we carry."

"Come on," encouraged Seebaer, "let's get moving."

Pieter moved up to the cliff as the fire raged, the bodies that remained after the storm beginning to burn, the fat within the bodies providing fuel for the flames and in an outstretched hand he offered Ariaen something which he did not expect. In his hand he held a pipe.

"For the tobacco you carry in that small box of yours," said Pieter half smiling, the dirty deed of setting light to the fire having been done. "You might like to clean it first."

"Thank you, Pieter," smiled Ariaen as he turned the pipe over in his hand, studying it closely, seeing whether or not it would hold up to being smoked. "It looks sound. I'll clean it tonight."

"You should consider yourself lucky that only a few other men amongst us smoke as you."

"I guess so," agreed Ariaen. "But share I must," and turned to glance upon the flames as they licked up the cliff's face and into the air.

Hendrik then stepped up from beyond some scrub and nonchalantly said, "It might concern some that the fire will attract the attention of the savages."

"My God," answered Ariaen with a little panic, "You're right."

"But if we are to signal a ship at a later date then I guess it's of little concern," and walked away, continuing on back to the campsite.

"That's the first, real, common sense thing I've heard him say," said Pieter, to Ariaen "and he just walked away before I could tell him so."

"Savage this, native that," shrugged Ariaen. "I guess we will encounter each other sooner or later. It won't make a great deal of difference... what do you think?"

"No, not really," answered Pieter. He looked over to where Wiebbe and Willem were standing. "They don't seem to care too much."

"Maybe they haven't given it much thought," replied Ariaen. "Or maybe they're concerned for one another. After all, Willem currently has needs, as does Wiebbe."

"Why, Wiebbe?"

"He and Dirck are our only real hope," said Ariaen. "They know more than the rest put together when it comes down to survival and the needs of the sick."

"Then maybe they should teach us."

Ariaen looked into Pieter's eyes, "Maybe we should be looking to the natives of this land. They've lived here for their entire lives. They're the ones that can save us; no one else."

"Hmmm, you're probably right," agreed Pieter.

"So... I know Hendrik smokes; I can see it in his teeth," stated Adrian. "Who's the other?"

"Dirck."

"What about Seebaer and the others?"

"I'm not too sure, but maybe you and I should just shut our mouths and keep it between just a few," said Pieter.

"No," said Ariaen. "I'll share... lead by example."

CHAPTER TWENTY-TWO

"It's a sorrowful sight... very depressing," said Pieter as he looked down upon the burning corpses, the flames leaping into the air.

"You're right," answered Hendrik and turned away, heading back to the small camp, to filter through what was left of the food, and he wasn't gone long before he screamed out a mass of obscenity in respect to what confronted him when he got there, for just beyond the fire, where the meat was supposed to be kept tightly bound with a cover and in the shade, he found it was bare to the air around.

The others came running, Willem following up the rear at a slow pace, feeling weak and mentally drained.

"What is it; what's the matter?" asked Ariaen as he drew alongside Hendrik, Marinus looking over from where he lay, half drowsed from slumber and finding it hard to see what was the matter.

"The meat," pointed Hendrik. "It's spoiled; every last chunk, strip, and bone."

A mass of flies of the likes they had not seen before had swarmed upon the meat, the cover to the prize having been dislodged by the wind earlier on and falling to the ground. There were ants in the thousands, lines upon lines of them, coming and going, a banquet ready for the taking.

"Maybe we can wash it," said Marinus, trying to help, hoping to contribute something to the group as opposed to laying there like a cripple, drawing his rations in water and food but performing no task or responsibility.

"Wash it!" cringed Hendrik. "Are you mad? It's contaminated."

"I'm afraid he's right," said Wiebbe.

"Of course I'm right," came Hendrik's familiar tone once more.

"We can't take a chance on it," said Wiebbe. "Willem has been bad and it could well be because of this meat. He's young and fragile, unable to take the abuses of disease as a fully grown man can. If nothing else, the sea has taught me that."

"Ah!" yelled Hendrik. "The boy, it's his fault. The meat was stored by his action, his responsibility. The fault is his."

Willem then stepped upon the small open area, the others surrounding the fire and the stored meat, the dislodged cover bearing all to the world, invitation for all the insects that roamed the land.

"It wasn't me," said Willem, a pleading look within his eyes. "I placed the cover upon it, I know I did."

"It's okay, Willem," consoled Pieter, "It's not your fault; it was the storm."

Hendrik fell upon his haunches and covered his face with his hands, "Blast, it. The boy should have checked it, thrice each morning, thrice each night; to double check is obviously not good enough."

"It's too late now," said Wiebbe.

"Yes," agreed Dirck as he moved over to Marinus, tired of the bickering. "Throw it into the sea and forget it. The last thing we need is to be divided by discontent, and to see this meat sitting there is a bad reminder."

CHAPTER TWENTY-THREE

Their faces were rather solemn, a little shellfish to be shared amongst them all. Hendrik stared at Willem from time to time, a snarl expressed, an upturned lip betraying his feelings, though little betrayal was required as Hendrik had offered his dissatisfaction earlier on.

The large fire was still burning although the flames were quite small when compared to before, the black smoke having subsided and the fat from the bodies, though little there seemed to be, turning the mass of flesh into a blackened mass of unrecognizable burnt bone and charcoal.

Seebaer was the first to be heard as he called out to the group, knowing he was close due to the disruption in the air caused by the heat from the fire. The others came suddenly after him, the wombat placed down for all to see.

"Seebaer," said Wiebbe, standing on his feet and greeting him with a slap on the shoulder, happy to see that all had returned safely, the fact that smiles upon their faces indicated good spirits, and he could see why.

"By, damn," said Ariaen. "What manner of creature is that?"

"I wish I knew," answered Seebaer. "We caught it this morning and have been carrying it ever since."

"We also saw the smoke from the fire," interrupted Jan, pushing into the conversation, cutting Ariaen off from making further comments. "I can only presume that Harmen was amongst those burnt in the fire; unless it was a signal for a passing ship, which I doubt considering that none of you are dancing upon the edge of the cliff."

"You're right," said Ariaen. "We burnt the dead; all of them."

"With or without sermon?"

"Without, Jan. Who here is a priest or other man of the cloth? No one, that's who."

"I would like to have said my goodbye before he was cast into the flame."

"It's never too late," said Ariaen, understanding the torments of friendship torn apart.

Jan looked around and stepped away, not another word passing his lips as he disappeared from view.

"So; what news do you have?" asked Pieter, changing the subject, bringing joy back into their world, even if briefly.

"No real news," said Seebaer. "We ran out of food and found it hard to continue under such trying conditions. We decided to return and have brought back this... thing, as you can see."

"We'll have to hang it," said Wiebbe.

"Not here," said Ariaen. "Seebaer, we've decided on a few changes to make our survival more comfortable and increase our chances of communication with the natives."

"Waste of time," said Hendrik, "if you ask me."

"It's necessary," said Adriane, standing up for Wiebbe and his plan. "We're going to maintain three campsites."

"Three," voiced Cornelis apprehensively. "We can't even manage to care for one; how are we going to manage three?"

"We have to try," said Wiebbe. "There's a good position a little further inland... not far. We can see the ocean from there; any passing ship will be easily spotted. A little past that and we'll have another, for the sick."

"The sick?" prodded Seebaer for confirmation.

"Willem fell ill last night," advised Wiebbe. "We don't know what caused it but it could have been the meat or something else he'd eaten."

Seebaer and the others having just returned looked to Willem who seemed well enough.

"He had a fever and stomach pain, felt very weak and seemed to forget himself for a while," continued Wiebbe. "He's better now, as you can see, so we know he doesn't have a disease or tropical fever."

Seebaer looked at Willem, "You look pale, too," he added.

"Even paler last night," said Wiebbe.

Seebaer took a pace forward, "Do you know what I think it is?"

Wiebbe was utterly flabbergasted, beside himself and in shock that Seebaer should happen upon the cause of Willem's discomfort and in a matter of seconds.

"I think he has Porphyria Variegate," concluded Seebaer. "I've seen it before, and it strikes mostly after childhood." He looked to Wiebbe and back to Willem. "Exactly as you say, the symptoms exactly. The more severe cases can suffer hallucinations, skin damage, diarrhoea, muscle weakness and seizures; sensitivity to sunlight, blistering of the skin and scarring. Fever and sweating is quite common. Willem; your family... does anyone suffer like this?"

"Yes," said Willem. "My mother suffers badly from hallucinations and pain, weakness and fever. She's a drunk and cares little for me. The doctors said what you just said... that name."

"Porphyria Variegate," said Seebaer.

"Yes, that's right," confirmed Willem.

"Well, I think that's your answer," said Seebaer.

"And what's the cure?" asked Wiebbe.

"There isn't one, but it can be helped," said Seebaer, though with little confidence.

"And how is that?" prodded Pieter for an answer, eager to help the boy under his care.

"Plenty of food."

Ariaen took no time in giving the orders, the overwhelming power of command flowing through him that second, to see to it that all was done to help Willem, "We do as suggested by Wiebbe. Wiebbe, show us all where the campsite is to be and then the hospital. Cornelis and Jan can carry Marinus, Dirck his things. Seebaer and Joannes, bring the... animal; we can set up the third sight and prepare our next meal immediately, for Willem's sake."

"Throw it on a fire as it is," interrupted Hendrik. "Why waste your energy cutting away the skin and draining the blood?"

"Because we know too little about the animals of this land and I see no good coming from supping on more blood than is necessary," advised Ariaen. "It's called farming, Hendrik, and besides, the skin can go towards making boots and a hat... or do you think we should throw all manner of material to the flame of a good fire?"

Hendrik didn't answer, he saw the error of his way and it was clear to him that the others had put more thought into the campsites than he had done, not to mention the preparation of the animal that he had overlooked.

"Let's get to work immediately and get Willem something good to eat," finished Ariaen. "We start trapping for more food as soon as we can but in the meantime we set up our campsites and get ready to eat."

Nothing further was said and the men set to duty, doing as they should do in order to survive. There was no more bickering, just hard work.

CHAPTER TWENTY-FOUR

By nightfall all had been secured: the three separate sites had been established, to some form of reasonable degree.

All of the survivors came together as darkness fell upon them, even Marinus was carried down to the main camp where the sea could be easily seen, carried upon a litter made from some wood from the Zuytdorp and some cloth.

The meat of the animal had been separated from the remains of the animal, innards discarded, thrown aside for the ants and flies to have their way with it, and the skin lay out upon the ground, pegged into place and stretched ready for further scraping. The ants clambered over it and they would remove all of the meat from the skin, and the stench of the remains would be buried later on when more time was made available for those manning the third site, but the time now was for a little celebration, to congratulate one another on what they had, so far, accomplished.

Each person held a plate of some description, whether it be made from wood or a large piece of bark, each filled with well cooked meat and fat. Willem wasted no time at all in having his fill and all around knew that from this day forth they would have to provide special care to Willem, to ensure he remained full of food and spared the more arduous chores availed by the group. Wiebbe could only think that the work the boy did earlier contributed to his falling sick, but he knew deep down that he wasn't to blame... Willem was simply unstoppable when it came to pulling his own weight but now that would have to change.

There was more eating than talking and for obvious reasons, for the group of survivors had been without a good meal for so long. Their main staple was shellfish of varying types, which was not always going to be available due to the weather – an alternative would have to be considered.

"Do you know something?" said Joannes. "I was thinking that we could build ourselves an oven, for smoking fish and drying meat. Jerky would serve us well at times when the weather proved too bad to scrounge. We can't stuff ourselves with food and then go days without."

"Especially not Willem," added Pieter.

"What about the natives?" prodded Dirck. "How do they survive?"

"Don't worry about them," said Jan. "They'd not go without."

"Which is why we should consider befriending them," said Ariaen.

"It's all well and good to be thinking along the lines of long-term survival," said Hendrik, "but I don't see how any of it is going to achieve anything. We should wait for a boat to come."

"And what if one doesn't?" said Dirck.

"Don't give me your defeatist attitude," spat Hendrik. "If a boat doesn't come then we build our own and set sail for Batavia."

"It's no good building a boat if it can't be launched, and we certainly can't build on the shoreline platform... the boat would be decimated within a day or two."

"But there is a site," said Hendrik. "I heard of it, just a few hundred yards away, to the south."

"Take a look, Hendrik," said Seebaer. "It's not good for launching. We're stuck here and that's all there is to it. Our only hope is that a ship will see our signal fire and launch a boat to save us. Other than that we are on our own."

Silence struck again and the meal was finished, it was then

that Ariaen pulled a pipe from within his tattered shirt pocket, "Do you see what was found by Pieter earlier on."

"Not much use without tobacco," said Hendrik.

"Which I have with me," said Ariaen as he pulled his tobacco box from within his blanket on which he was seated, "right here."

"By God," said Hendrik, "Real tobacco.

"How much is there?" asked Cornelis.

"Not much," said Ariaen, "but enough to satisfy us each night this week and even the next. If we spare it properly I can see it lasting a good four weeks, at least. But it depends on one thing... who here would like to smoke?"

Voices were raised as were arms, five individuals offering themselves to their luxury of indescribable pleasure and relaxation; six including Ariaen.

"We shall have one pipe a night, to be shared between us, and no more," said Ariaen. "Do you agree?"

"Agreed, agreed!" came the response, all but Hendrik voicing his anxiousness to the restriction.

"Do you think you are in more need than another?" asked Ariaen.

"No," said Hendrik, his feathers ruffled. "I don't," and then, "just light the damn thing so that we can get it started."

And the joyous song of satisfaction went up again and a single pipe of tobacco was surrendered to its ashes, the last wisps of smoke filling the air around the camp, all breathing a sigh of relief in the feeling that it provided them. Even those that didn't smoke enjoyed the smell of smoke, the reminder that they were still a part of civilization, even if thousands of miles from home and shipwrecked upon a strange and seemingly uninhabitable land.

"Shall we consider our order of business?" asked Wiebbe of the others, looking at Ariaen for his input.

"Yes indeed, let's deliberate," said Ariaen. "From our earlier conversations it is clear that a ship may very well pass by this way in three days. We should make haste tomorrow and ensure that we are ready with a signal fire within two. Every able-bodied man should assist in this, except Willem and one other. These two should remain at the third camp and prepare traps, try and make a few weapons such as a spear; like we have seen the natives carry. We also need to consider what means of contact we intend to use with the natives."

"I don't think that will be a problem," said Jan. "They will show themselves soon enough; in that I'm quite confident. They won't shy away too long."

"I agree," said Pieter," but it wouldn't do any harm to keep our eyes open and to make the first approach towards friendship."

"We need a gift," said Joannes, "something to offer them."

"And what do you suggest?" asked Hendrik.

"I don't know."

"Food," said Willem. "Everyone here will need food, even if they are natives of this land. The others we have seen were carrying spears, so unless they feared others that they are at war with, they must be on the lookout for food."

"Stands to reason," said Pieter with a smile. "I think we should make an oven for drying meat as soon as we possibly can, and there is no better place than the third campsite, nearer the plains where the natives have been spotted earlier."

"And how do we know they're friendly?" asked Hendrik in his sour way once more.

"We don't," said Willem, "but we can smile and make an offering to them. If they were going to kill us then they would have done it already."

"Maybe," said Hendrik, "maybe not. Only time will tell. But I tell you all this, right now, that I don't care for these schemes of yours, none of them. I would much prefer to build a boat...

and maybe tomorrow I'll start."

"Hendrik," said Ariaen, "so long as you don't take the wood we use on the signal fire, you can take what you want from the Zuytdorp."

"And when my boat is ready for the sea I shall only take those that make apologies and pay for their place," said Hendrik, full of spite.

"Maybe we should make you pay for the tobacco, Hendrik, and the place you keep beside the fire."

And seeing the error of his way, Hendrik moved off towards where the cliff top looked out over the sea, the clear of the night growing colder but the wind having died down to practically nothing.

CHAPTER TWENTY-FIVE

Over the next two days all went reasonably well. No natives had been spotted and Marinus appeared to be healing rather well, considering the manner by which the splints had been applied.

The traps made by those at the third campsite were rather petty and proved to be ineffective, so shellfish was the main source of their nourishment, although several large fish were caught on the shoreline platform, separated from the sea by small rock pools. But the sea was too dangerous to remain next to for too long, with waves casting themselves upon anyone who went down to the Zuytdorp to look for salvage and wood. Most of what was carried by the Zuytdorp was either washed out to sea or if heavy enough had sunk to the bottom and lay in wait for future treasure hunters. It was here that the coins were found, but as they offered little to the men who had survived they were left where they lay, only several handfuls taken as reminders of a world lost more than anything else.

Willem had prevented further attacks by remaining well fed when compared to the others, in spite of what Hendrik had to say in regards to having less, and his workload was down to non-essential duty where he performed menial tasks for those that were hard at work improving on their living condition such as sanitation, the gathering of fuel for the signal fire and in constant forage for food.

Two signal fires were made, the second not too close to the first so as to be ignited when one was put to flame, but close enough so that the second fire could be struck if the first failed to flare properly, or if it burnt out and further signalling was required.

Tinder was maintained at the main camp which could see far and wide across the expanse of the sea to the west, kept as dry as possible in a small barrel taken from the wreck, a shelter above the main fire provided sufficient protection against the wind and rain, though rain hadn't been seen since the last downpour, and each knew that the construction of the site might not stand up to a storm as ferocious as the one that had wrecked them upon the shore. For a better and more permanent construction the campsite would have to be moved in land, away from the cliff and wind, to a place where there was sufficient protection offered by tree trunks and other natural sources within the lay of the land.

The availability of water was also a concern for most as it was apparent that the gully to their flank, which drained into the sea, was not flowing. When rain was prevalent then it might flow substantially enough to provide a good source of fresh water, but this couldn't be guaranteed. In respect to this another barrel, damaged along the top third of its circumference, was used to store water, set up so that it would catch any rain that fell from the cloth that they used as part of their shelter, the barrel half buried in the ground to prevent it from toppling over.

It seemed that everything was in order until on the morning of the day that the Kockenge was expected to appear somewhere upon the horizon, for on this morning the unexpected occurred.

CHAPTER TWENTY-SIX

11th June.

Hendrik was hard at work, fighting against the thrashing sea as the waves threw themselves upon him, one after the other.

He had commenced to gather good wood for the building of a boat, a boat that would take him to Batavia, or in the least, towards any passing ship that neared the coast. It was simply a matter of time, or so he told himself, until a ship passed this way, and it was up to him to ensure that he survived.

He maintained a steady watch towards the west, keeping a fitful open eye for any sail that might break the horizon with squares of white, flapping cloth; not that it mattered any, for the boat he intended to throw into the sea wasn't even made yet, not even started; all he had was a mass of wood.

In the least he provided the other survivors with pieces of wood that didn't serve his purpose and although these were rather small and still quite soaked, it was the only way in which Hendrik felt he could make amends for his wretched way. He knew deep down that he was pushing the survivors to hate him more and more each passing day, but he couldn't help it; it was his way. So he cast his thoughts aside and continued with his work whilst above him, overlooking the sea to the west, the others continued to put together their signal fire, placing tinder and other small bushes, scrub and branches beneath a pyramid of heavier wood, with a barrel of drier material close at hand for the ignition of the fire when the time arose.

All felt that the calculations made earlier were correct and that today was the day that a sighting would be made, but how close the Kockenge was to sail was unknown; if it was day then it might stay far out to sea, and might not even be seen; if by night then they would have to rely on a good moon or noise from the ship itself to know it was even there.

The bells, bells upon the deck, that's what they would listen for. The lookout at night would most definitely hear any noise from the ship, surely, in particular when taking into consideration the direction of the wind.

Night, however, was a long time off as it was currently just after noon, lunch having been missed by all except Willem, who ate a small handful of shellfish, and didn't feel the better for it. It was his inner ambition to help the survivors, not to impede on their desperate plight; his being no less desperate. He was a child turning into a man, as indicated by his Porphyria Variegate. He knew full well that he had to eat as did the others that fed him, but he couldn't help feeling as though he was a burden upon them, just another inconvenience to be suffered on top of everything else that they had to suffer, and all the time that he put food into his mouth he felt worse and worse for it.

Dirck took time off from the parties at work during the day to check on Marinus, even though Willem had made this one of his sole duties. It was simply another stab in the heart for Willem who felt that he hadn't yet been fully accepted, for if he had been accepted then Dirck would have left Marinus in his care and not troubled himself with taking time off from the work that was urgently required.

Dirck knew there was no ulterior motive for his attending Marinus, though this was hard to prove to Willem. He'd been looking after the man since they first arrived, where Wiebbe commenced to undertake other duties and leaving him to attend to the sick as they dwindled in number before their very eyes. It

117

would be too easy to ward off the responsibility to Willem, as Wiebbe had awarded the responsibility off to Dirck; he refused to allow this to happen. Dirck had sworn to himself that he would attend Marinus until he was fit and well, walking upon his own two feet and without need of further assistance; there was simply no way that Dirck was going to offload the pressure of the job to Willem. Dirck, a man of faith and great inspiration, sitting there and drawing a dirty sleeve across his lips, a little blood having come from his gums. He ignored the signature of blood and continued with his work.

As for Wiebbe, he felt more in command than a healer or comforter of the sick. To Wiebbe their very survival depended on good decisions being made. He looked at himself as being a part of the council, a council of several men that made the decisions for the remainder of their group. There was himself and Ariaen and Pieter, each and every one a good man with the brains to organise and see things through. With a council of three the others were more likely to listen and pay heed to the suggestions that were made and the decisions finally decided. The council weaved their magic rather masterfully, corrupting the minds of the others into accepting their judgement without even realising that judgement had been passed, and even more profound was the fact that the council didn't fully understand that they were indeed being manipulative... it was simply the way of the council, a system that was jostled into position and worked well. It was more a case of sheer luck than anything else.

Ariaen and Pieter were happy with their roles within the group, Ariaen as leader and Pieter as an advisor: a right-hand man with plenty of good ideas. Pieter had come from a good background where family issues were more important than most other things in life, a passion for living that his mother cast upon him, passions that his father seemed to wish see destroyed, proved by his pushing Pieter, as a child, into working his mind, to pry out an existence in an insane world, to make him stronger on the inside. Pieter never reflected upon it much, never deliberating on the subject openly, but had been rewarded by his parents actions by instilling self-confidence and the will to work a solution through and through until the end result was worthy to be praised. He was only held back by Ariaen whose very presence seemed to shower Pieter with an invisible blanket or shroud, Ariaen shining through as the decision maker of the group through the combined motion of the council. Ariaen: a man of distinction, a man of healing, a man of good standing when on board the Zuytdorp and now washed up on land. It was his easy-going nature that made it for him, his very character that showed all around him that he knew what he was talking about. How could such a man be refused an open ear, a friendly smile, and a nod of the head?

And what of Hendrik? He knew how to scoff and refuse.

And so Hendrik continued to plod away on the gathering of good wood until that hour after midday when a freak wave towered out of the sea and fell upon him, bashing him hard against a rock. His vision blurred with the knock to his head, a cloud moving across him, a permanent covering; death. It was almost immediately after that that the alarm was raised and men appeared upon the cliff to look down upon the body of the man they knew as an individual, being washed out to sea, a burial that would see his body eaten by creatures of the Indian Ocean.

Seebaer was just near the edge of the cliff when the incident occurred; all he could do was stand there and watch. It was as though his voice had been stolen from him, despite the fact that the wave was too loud, too large, and too fast. Hendrik was too busy to notice anything out of the ordinary and any effort on Seebaer's part to draw the attention of Hendrik to the wave would have been futile. His jaw simply dropped when he saw the wave bury Hendrik, the lifeless body coming to surface momentarily as the water then cascaded away from the shoreline platform, another coming in to carry the body beneath the surging waves, the body showing itself from time to time before finally disappearing for good, never to be seen again.

Hendrik wasn't that much of a friend to Seebaer, but he was a survivor and that meant they were brothers of the same ordeal. Each and every one of them needed to look out for the other, otherwise they were all doomed to the same fate, be it buried by the sea, bitten by a snake, or carried away by the natives of this barren land to be cooked upon an open fire and eaten.

Joannes, Cornelis and Jan were the first to be at Seebaer's side, looking down upon Hendrik for that last dying minute. What could be said? Very little. It was simply amazing how quickly the waves had grabbed hold of Hendrik and taken him away, as though he were connected to some invisible rope and being drawn away by an invisible ship.

But they continued to watch even after he'd disappeared as they scanned the ocean for a final glimpse of their friend, and then Cornelis, his young eye seeing something on the horizon, gave an emotional leap of joyous salvation, springing the news upon all around that a ship could be seen coming towards them, nothing more than a little scratch in the distance where the sea met the sky, and then it disappeared.

"I don't see anything," said Jan with such hope in his voice that he nearly fell over through careless shifting of his feet.

"It was there," came the exasperation from Cornelis. "I swear to God that I saw a ship."

"It must be the Kockenge," voiced Ariaen as he came running up, confused between the sad look of Joannes as he looked down into the surf and the overcrowded joy of the other three. "What's wrong, Joannes? If it's a ship, then we're saved."

"Hendrik has gone, taken by the sea," he answered.

"It's a miracle, is what it is," said Seebaer. "If it wasn't for the wave that took Hendrik's life then we wouldn't be looking at the ship at this moment."

"But I don't see it," repeated Jan.

"Nor do I," came Pieter's voice as he too moved up behind the others.

"Just look and wait," urged Cornelis. "It's disappeared... there it is!"

"I see it!" yelled Jan.

"Me too!" came a frantic call from Pieter.

And before they knew it everyone upon the cliff top had seen the ship in the distance, disappearing and then coming to view, the waves obscuring their sight of the ship from time to time.

It was sheer jubilation, a great relief, as though all of their burdens had been removed from them; but Ariaen was more sober in thought and gave the command to set light to the signal fire, his mind quite open to the reality of the situation and that the ship might not see them at all. It was so far away and could turn to the north at any minute.

Seebaer and his three closest companions set themselves to task and the signal fire was soon ablaze; Pieter had alerted the others to the rear of the approaching vessel and then returned to stand by Ariaen when he noticed that his expression was rather lax, not a crease to be seen, neither a smile nor a grim expression being painted, just a simple, sober look.

"What is it, Ariaen," asked Pieter.

"If we can see the ship then the ship can see the coast," he answered nonchalantly, "which means that they will turn to the north at any minute. I'm sure as sure can be that there will be many eyes cast in our direction, but the fire might not be seen. Men will be resting below deck or busy upon it. There is no navigational reference in this region that will confirm their position so the lookout will have his eyes on the north, looking for the bay which I've calculated as being around fifty miles to the north. Aye, I see the look in your eye. I've taken many notes on the layout of the stars, as others have done. You know as much as I do about our predicament. The way men work on the sea is one of question upon question, confirmation needed on their position; how deep is the sea; how much till they bottom out when approaching land; what's the best speed that can be maintained? Our best hope lies in the reality that the smoke might be seen, if we are lucky; but no call to action will be taken upon us until they reach Batavia. Only then will they learn of our disappearance; only then will they consider the signal we make today as a signal from the survivors of the good ship Zuytdorp."

Ariaen looked around at the others, some having stopped in their tracks to look upon him. "Light the second fire, immediately. Our only hope lies in the hope that they will see us and report it to the officials in Batavia on learning of our failure to show."

And the men worked as they had never worked before, setting light to the second signal fire, running for scrub and anything else that would burn and send plumes of smoke into the sky.

"If the natives don't know we're here," said Joannes, "they certainly do now."

The smoke was thick for a few minutes and then quickly died away, a thick haze of rising heat replacing the black clouds of the furnace below. Was it enough to alert the Kockenge; was it enough to kick a seaman in the head, to bring a rescue ship over the coming months? Only time would tell.

And that was the first and last ship they saw. The Oostersteyn on 15th June, Zuyderbeeck on 24th, Belvliet on 25th, Popkensburg on 29th, and then the Corsloot and Oude Zyp on 5th July; all had bypassed them, either by day or by night, too far out to be seen or passing too far to the north. Salvation wasn't to come their way, not to be a part of their lives. And so the signal fires sat at the ready until such a time that each pile was steadily reduced to help maintain the three fires in the campsites they had established.

CHAPTER TWENTY-SEVEN

12th July.

They all sat around the camp fire of the main site where vigil upon the sea wasn't made available during the day, the other two temporarily abandoned as their purpose was superseded by the requirement for comradeship and togetherness.

They were well into the winter months and although rain was not altogether a common occurrence it did provide them with the ability to maintain stock levels on their water supply. As for food, that was another story. They had learnt to set traps for the slower animals and never shied away from testing the stench of a reasonably fresh carcass for edibility. Shellfish was always there but little else attained. Beetles and other small grubs were occasionally mixed in with other sources of nourishment but this was always accompanied by a sour look upon faces and never eaten alone.

Willem had suffered from time to time, minor attacks of Porphyria Variegate coming to air, but never serious enough to see his basic health levels decline. At any time that an attack arrived out of the blue the men would give up most of their meal in order for Willem to go with a few extra days of nourishment, and it seemed to help. It was never questioned, but was a simple act of brotherly love. But was it simple, to give your life away for someone else to eat, an act of courage to best all acts.

Marinus was forever in recovery. His ribs had seemingly healed but there was plenty of pain in his left arm, something he often joked about: still having the ability to wipe his own backside.

"And what about you, Jan?" asked Pieter as Willem ate from a bark bowl to his right. "What are you contemplating?"

"Oh; nothing, really. I was just thinking about these shoes of mine. They're damn near the end of their life," and Jan looked down upon the big toes of both feet, showing through breaks in the leather, exposed to the torments of the cold. "I nearly burnt my feet the other night, soles bare to the flames of our fire."

"Wrap another blanket around your feet," suggested Seebaer. "You'll do even better if you keep dry."

A few of the men looked around; they didn't have spare blankets.

"I was thinking of getting some shoes made from one of those furs, like what you and Marinus have," said Jan to Seebaer.

"You can have the next one," said Ariaen, seeing that Jan had the biggest need.

"Thank you, Ariaen. I appreciate that."

"What other needs do we currently have?" asked Ariaen of all of them, "apart from food."

"We still need something for scurvy," said Wiebbe, thinking of Dirck Fret, the man so ready to avail himself to the aid of others that he had neglected the effects of what he had suffered: his bleeding from the lips being the first sign, his death being the last.

They all knew that Wiebbe was right. They needed to desperately find some form of nourishment other than meat and shellfish. Roots were needed, some form of edible fruit. But what did they know of this land other than what they had stumbled across by accident. What was edible and what was not?

"Dirck was a good man," voiced Marinus as he rubbed his arm, the pain showing upon his face, the joining of the two bones not being as perfect as it should. "I feel a little responsible for his death."

"Don't be," said Wiebbe. "He wouldn't have wanted you to think like that."

"He served me well," added Marinus.

"He served us all well," said Ariaen. "It wasn't your fault he died of scurvy. He must have been under its spell well before he arrived at Table Bay."

"He was transferred from another ship," said Cornelis. "He'd only be ashore one or two days, barely enough to fill up on fruit or cabbage."

"Ah, cabbage," said Wiebbe, changing the subject, pulling everyone from the misery of Dirck's death just days before, where scurvy had taken its toll on his body, killing him gradually over the past weeks where pain got the better of him. "That's what we need right now, something green."

"There's nothing here but scrub," said Seebaer. "What are we to do?"

Pieter looked at the others, "You all know what we need to do. The winter, so far, has brought little rain, the summer months will be even worse. Is it no surprise that the natives we've seen to date wore no clothing. We have no good food, and over the coming months, as we enter into next summer, we'll have no water to speak of. We have no way of surviving here without the help of the natives."

Again the same tune.

There was silence then and all dwelt upon the comments. They'd spoken a little on the natives several times over the past few days, in wake of Dirck's death.

"I think it's time we voted on the matter," said Ariaen. "All those in favour of making contact with the natives, raise your hand."

Some were slower than others, but all eventually had their

arm held up high, a little pessimism seeping into Jan.

"But one thing must be said," announced Seebaer. "We must first wait until the end of August. If no ship has returned by then, then we should proceed."

"No," said Cornelis. "That's too late. We need to act now. I agree we should remain here, in this camp until, well, maybe even the beginning of summer, or when the water has run out, but contact must be made. Scurvy is treacherous to us all and Willem is also suffering and on a regular basis. We need help now."

Yes, the same tune, putting off a good endeavour.

"Good," said Ariaen. "So let's consider it. We'll remain here until summer or when the water runs dry, but contact must be made."

"And what are we going to barter?" asked Joannes. "Why would the natives of this land want to help us?"

"Well... we have nothing, really," answered Pieter. "Maybe some coins from the wreck."

"Let's not consider that, the sea's far too unpredictable," rushed Wiebbe. "We can't risk anyone getting killed over a few coins. They're not going to get us anywhere."

"We have nothing," concluded Ariaen. "All we can do is show good intention and hope for the best. I doubt for a minute they're aggressive otherwise we'd be dead already."

"He's right," defended Marinus. "Jan saw another one just a few days ago."

"Yes," admitted Jan, reminding all of the encounter, "He was quite far out and all he could do was stand there, watching me, clad in fur. I don't like them. That's the conclusion I've come to"

"A fur?" questioned Ariaen.

"Maybe I forgot to mention it," admitted Jan, "but yes, he had something on, something to keep him warm, I'm sure of it; but he was a fair distance away." He looked around the camp fire. "It was raining, he was standing there and then he walked off. He wasn't afraid, either, you could tell this by his leisurely walk. He just kept on walking into the landscape and disappeared."

"Clothing," repeated Wiebbe.

"They're not animals," said Ariaen, unconsciously scratching at the huge scar on his head where the bandage once rested, his wound having healed sufficiently for the cloth to be removed. "They must have lived on this land for many years. They know the way of the land. They know what is good to eat and what is not. We'll die if we stay here and do nothing. I'm growing tired of waiting."

"Let me take a party of men out into the east," volunteered Seebaer. "Let me do this for all of us."

Ariaen was silent for a moment and then nodded his head, "Very well. Take as much water as you can carry and eat well before you depart. How many days—?"

"Just a few," interrupted Seebaer. "No more than four."

"Very well," agreed Ariaen as he reached for his tobacco box and pipe. "I have enough for one more smoke, a large one to do us all. Let's finish what we have."

Seebaer, Cornelis and Jan all smiled.

Marinus then turned the question to Seebaer, "Who do you want to take with you?"

"Cornelis, Jan and Joannes."

Marinus then took the fur shoes from his feet and handed them to Jan, "Take these; I'll get the next ones that come along."

"Thank you, Marinus," came the most sincere gratitude Marinus had ever heard.

Marinus managed to get Jan's shoes on his feet without too much trouble and felt immediately the discomfort and cold due to the open toes being fed to the air, the leather worn so incredulously that holes larger than several coins were on display, almost half the front portion to each shoe missing. They would serve their purpose until such a time that something else could be gained and taken advantage of.

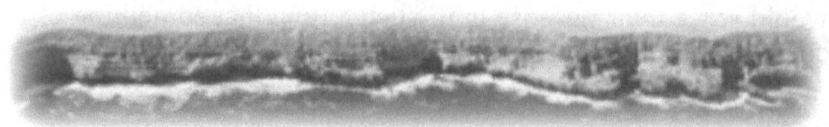

CHAPTER TWENTY-EIGHT

The group of four, under no charge except a comfortable leadership role being displayed by Seebaer, departed after having had enough to eat to satisfy the early beginnings of their journey, this being the first time in more than four weeks that the men had eaten more than their fair share and certainly more than Willem. They felt a little uncomfortable taking the source of the boy's good health away from him but they would probably not get another opportunity to eat again for several days.

They carried a receptacle each, differing in purpose and shape, which carried water, and although it was still winter and rain could be expected at any time their overall experience showed the land to be a dry place and very unforgiving. The fact that they were able to rely on a rock hole as a water source didn't distract their knowledge from the fact that summer would see them without such a valuable resource. Many times individuals had heard, or experienced directly, of the blistering heat of the region whilst sailing past on their way to Batavia, but none of that could experience them for the reality of what was to come as the sun commenced to grow higher in the sky as the months unfolded before them.

Between the four of them they also carried a blanket each, a little sail cloth, to be used as a shelter, and several long pieces of rope.

They hadn't travelled far beyond the extent of the third camp when they saw a familiar sight, a kangaroo hopping away followed shortly thereafter by two more, and within minutes an emu crossed their path. It was a common occurrence to them now, nothing out of the ordinary. They had even spoken of trying to catch an emu for food but all attempts to think of a beneficial way had evaded them.

More than three quarters of the day had fallen behind them before they encountered their first contact with the natives and that was only in the form of an old fireplace, a hearth which had been abandoned long ago. It was easy to see that a smaller animal than those they had seen during their time on land had been eaten, for several bones sat white and dry, having been cleaned well by ants and the weather.

There was a little consideration by them to employ the site as a camp but with just under half a day still remaining before nightfall and no water or food source having been encountered, it was decided to continue on a little longer before bedding down for the night beneath a blanket and sail cloth.

The solemn look upon each of their faces told the story of the hard slog onwards, even in winter the land took its toll upon them. Their food intake over the coming weeks had been scarcely enough to carry them forward in their effort to survive, but to exert themselves upon the current task was starting to look foolish, the very nature of their task sinking further and further from them as an appropriate means by which to secure longevity.

Now, just two hours short of the sun disappearing on the horizon, the day's trek had come to an end.

"I don't know if I can continue like this for much longer," said Joannes and at 37 years of age was starting to show the wear of anxiety and exertion upon his face, the only real non-smoker amongst the small group so much less affected by the stresses of the situation.

Seebaer stopped dead in his tracks, just behind Cornelis, who, being the youngest of the group, had pressed ahead.

"Cornelis; wait," stammered Seebaer. He turned to the other two behind him. "Let's camp here for the night. I can't take much more and we should try and find something to eat."

Cornelis said not a word and moved back a few dozen feet to join his comrades, who fell upon the hard floor of the sandplains, exhausted and nearly at a loss for words except for an unsavoury comment for the land upon which they had struggled to comprehend.

"Doesn't this place ever change?" asked Jan of the others.

"You came this way before, as did all of us," said Cornelis of Jan. "What did you see then?"

"Yes, the same as what we saw now," said Jan. "It's the same, no matter where you go. Sure, the scenery might change a little but for the most part it is dry and uninhabitable."

"Which is why it's important to make good with the natives," said Joannes.

"No good can come of the natives," said Jan.

"Then why are you here?" asked Joannes.

"Here or there, what does it matter?" replied Jan. "The inevitable will happen sooner or later. We'll all die on this damn land."

"Don't speak like that, Jan," insisted Seebaer. "There is always hope."

"Hope didn't help Harmen," continued Jan of his argument.

"Where there is God, there is hope," said Seebaer, but he didn't really believe it; he didn't really believe that any good could come from trying to befriend the natives, but he tried to agree with the others.

"Yes, well," said Jan with upturned eyes. "If ever there was a Garden of Eden, this is not it. God has nothing good in store for us."

"We're alive," said Seebaer.

"But for how long?" asked Jan.

'Why don't we try and find something to eat?" suggested Cornelis. "I'll take a look around whilst you set up camp."

"Very well," surrendered Jan.

Cornelis exchanged glances with Joannes and they both moved away from Seebaer and Jan. They would circle the area and find something for them all. They had about two hours of searching by Cornelis' calculation and should be able to scrounge something up... he was determined.

CHAPTER TWENTY-NINE

The dark of the sky had started to move quite rapidly around them, howling in the distance shaking both Seebaer and Jan awake. They'd fallen asleep shortly after the shelter had been erected.

"That's close," said Jan.

"Too close," agreed Seebaer as he looked around. "Where are Cornelis and Joannes?"

Jan looked around and fear gripped him. He knew that no good could come of the enterprise.

"Cornelis..! Joannes!" yelled Jan, several dozen birds in a nearby tree taking flight into the evening air, a band of orange spanning the horizon from north to south. "Cornelis..! Joannes!"

They both listened but nothing was heard, no reply, nothing but an overture of birds, insects and the howling of a dog.

"That damn beast isn't far," said Seebaer. "I saw one the other week, a great reddish-brown animal looking directly at me whilst I cooked upon the camp fire."

"Which fire?"

"The preparation camp. I think the smell of fresh meat must have drawn him in."

"Are they big?" asked Jan.

"Big enough," answered Seebaer. "It doesn't take much of a wolf to bring down a man. Cornelis..! Joannes!"

"Maybe they're lost."

Seebaer stood there silently and listened with his entire might, "They aren't answering. They must be out of range."

"What should we do?"

"We'll have to try and get some rest, take turns maintaining watch," Seebaer looked into Jan's eyes. "We'll get some firewood and see what we can do with the tinderbox Ariaen gave us."

"I only hope we live to be able to give it back to him."

"Don't talk like that, Jan. Nothing good comes of it."

Jan considered it for a moment, the way in which he always turned to the negative.

"A fire, Jan; that's our priority at the moment."

CHAPTER THIRTY

"Did you hear that?" asked Cornelis as he loaned his ear to the sound so far away.

"It's just a dog," said Joannes. "It's far too far away to worry about. I can hardly hear it. I'm more concerned about being lost."

"Impossible, Joannes," insisted Cornelis, "We can't get lost. All we need to do is to turn west and head towards the sea."

"That's over a day's walk and we don't have any water," pointed out Joannes. "Why did we leave the water behind? We only had to bring a little."

"Joannes, listen; even if we were in the middle of a hot summer's day, I'm sure that we would be able to make it back to the cliff if we had to, but we only have to go back as far as the others."

"I'm sure you're right, but even they seem so far away. So what shall we do?"

"We'll have to stay here the night and try and find our way back in the morning."

"Very well; as you wish."

"The tinderbox would be like gold at the moment," said Cornelis as he sat down upon the hard ground.

"You know something strange?" said Joannes. "I feel tired, so very tired, and yet I don't think I can sleep. The exhaustion I feel right now is the worst I've felt since we've been here."

"We'll just sit and talk awhile, listen to the land, see what it has to say," said Cornelis.

"Yes, I think..." and Joannes' jaw dropped sharply as he looked up and beyond where Cornelis was seated.

Cornelis had a look of bewilderment and froze there on the spot. He felt within him that he knew what it was that had drawn Joannes' attention. His eyes darted from left to right, looking upon more than one thing.

"There's someone behind me, isn't there, Joannes?"

"Yes," replied Joannes. "Please don't move quickly, for there are six natives standing behind you and each is carrying a spear."

"Looking for food," Cornelis said blankly, unable to think of anything else to say.

"Probably," answered Joannes, thinking nothing more than their immediate fate, "and it seems that they've found it."

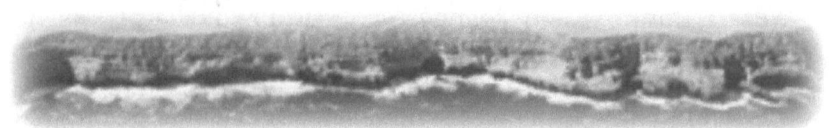

CHAPTER THIRTY-ONE

The night had been long for both Jan and Seebaer who had taken turns to remain awake, concerned for the welfare of their comrades and of course their own. The fire remained reasonably well lit even though there seemed little need for it.

The two men tried effortlessly one more time to call their friends home and after another two hours of sitting and waiting, wandering around the camp fire and looking off into the distance, they decided to return to the others.

It was quite obvious to them both that the other two would quickly come to their senses and head towards the west, soon to find their way home; and that in itself was strange, to think of this as their home, nothing more than a campsite near the edge of a cliff.

The embers of the fire weren't doused and Jan and Seebaer gathered their things and prepared for the move back. The move was going to be harder than the day before as they now had more to carry, with the extra blankets, water and shelter.

The sheer effort in maintaining a reasonable pace was shattering to say the least, the exhaustion from the walk taking its toll on both the men, in particular Jan. Seebaer had removed a little of the encumbrance which his friend had to suffer and carried it for him as the last thing he wanted was for anything to be left behind, to allow anything to be swallowed up by the sandplains and lost forever. Their very livelihood depended on the comforts and warmth gained by the little things in life and all that they possessed was in some small way a tool by which

N.B.J.Clayton

survival was made all the easier to achieve.

The sun was hotter on this day than any of the days over the past few weeks and it seemed that they might be in for an early summer, or a very hot one, but as learned men go they did not know of the countries weather patterns, but a constant reminder of the weather was written all around them, a reminder from which they couldn't escape. The land around them seemed worthless beyond all contemplation, the ground unable to offer a single thing of use or worth. But what the untrained eye failed to see was a land of great offering, many gifts going unnoticed by the Dutch, much food and water being missed by them all. In so many ways the land they walked upon was filled to the brim with food and water, all it took was many years of hard living to uncover, and that was something they did not have.

Again the day grew long and commenced to draw to a close but not before the two men could hear the familiar sound of the sea breaking its back against the shoreline platform of where the wreck of the Zuytdorp had commenced to disappear, the ship no longer resembling anything but a reminder of the misery delivered them all.

They literally staggered in on the others, Ariaen and Pieter being the first on their feet to provide assistance, the crackling of the fire before them drowning out the approach of the weary men, their throats dry and lips cracking, not a sound coming from either of them.

Willem scrambled to give aid but was quickly ordered to throw some food upon the fire, a small bandicoot caught that afternoon along with another which they had already eaten, the skins already pinned at the third site and away from their main shelter. Marinus dragged out a water container for each of the men to drink from on seeing that the water containers swinging from the hung shoulders of Jan and Seebaer were truly empty.

"Where's Cornelis and Joannes?" asked Ariaen.

139

"They're gone," answered Seebaer through cracked lips, barely audible but understood.

"Let them sit and drink," urged Pieter, "they're thirsty."

"You're right," agreed Ariaen and saw to it that nothing further was asked of them until they were ready.

Several mouthfuls of water later and after a deep breath, Seebaer broke the news all were eager to hear, "They're lost."

"Both of them?" asked Marinus.

"Do you see them with us?" spat Jan in sarcasm.

"I'm sorry," said Marinus and sat back down.

"Forget it," said Wiebbe.

"Where did you lose them?" asked Ariaen as he helped Seebaer with a little more water, looking to Willem as he turned the meat upon the fire.

"Last night," answered Seebaer. "We'd been walking almost all day, much further than Jan and Harmen. We had several hours before nightfall and Cornelis took Joannes with him to search the immediate area for water and food. Me and Jan fell asleep and when we woke, just at dusk, we saw that the others hadn't returned. We called them but to no avail. That night we maintained a watch and by morning decided there was nothing for it but to return," said Seebaer, the look in his eye showing how he'd wished that he could have done more. "We had to return." He kicked out at the dirt. "This sodden place is like hell on earth. There's no place worse, I'm sure of it."

Pieter then broke the silence, "Do you think they're dead?" he asked no one in particular.

"Time will tell," said Ariaen soberly. "If we don't hear from them over the next few days then we'll have to assume the worst. As Seebaer has said, this place is unforgiving."

"Maybe it is just that; unforgiving," agreed Pieter, "but it can be tamed."

"No," said Seebaer, "it won't be us who is taming it, but 'it'

140

will be taming us."

"Seebaer is right," surrendered Wiebbe, sucking his lips into his mouth and contemplating the facts. "We have to learn to live with the land, not the land with us."

"I thought that's what we were doing," said Jan, "trying to live with the land."

"No," said Wiebbe as he looked at Pieter. "We've been surviving on it, not melding with it. We have to become one with the land."

"What!" said Seebaer, "and become a savage?"

"Your so-called savages have lived on this land for as long as we've been sailing past it, and probably for a lot longer than that; maybe since Christ himself did walk the earth."

"No," disagreed Marinus. "Where are their houses, where are their accomplishments?"

"Maybe the land doesn't permit it," answered Pieter.

"I agree…. maybe it's for us to learn the ways of the land, by trying harder than we have before," said Wiebbe.

"I thought that's what we were trying to do, as civilized men, doing what needs to be done in order to survive," said Seebaer as he reflected upon the last few days and the exploration of the north. "We've been to the south, north and the east, and nothing has been found. Limited I agree, but still we endeavoured and made that asserted effort."

"It's not enough," said Wiebbe. "We have to do more. We have to make contact with the natives and we have to do it soon. When winter has gone and the last of the storms has passed this way the days will become hot and the ground crack from the heat. It will be like walking across the face of an anvil. Look around you; all of you. This land doesn't know anything but the harsh realities of life. I've seen other lands which have succumbed to the torments of heat upon heat, upon heat. I have seen other lands which have been spared no remorse, where the sun during the day was hot enough to melt the mind of a man in just a few hours. But I have never seen a land like this where the ground has been so savagely mistreated by the hand of God, where not a single flower can blossom nor a bee gathers nectar. We have to act. Summer will be upon us sooner than we think. We have to prepare ourselves for the worst by attempting to sojourn for a while in the best comfort we can scrounge."

"And what makes you think we're not here permanently, permanently incarcerated?" scoffed Seebaer. "To die right on this spot."

"Because I'll always maintain a little dignity and confidence; I'll always hold onto the hope within me," answered Wiebbe. "If I lose that, I lose everything."

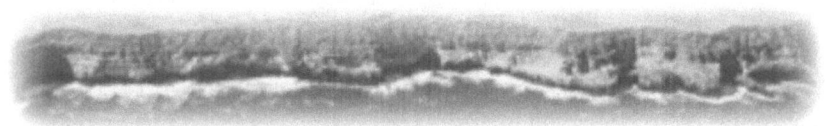

CHAPTER THIRTY-TWO

18th July.

The weather remained rather moderate over the coming days, a little rain falling upon the coast but not enough to fill the gullies with running water. A few opportunities to catch food passed their way but it was rather a case of too little, as it always was, and there was no choice that they had in regards to what they could eat, there was no choice when it came to suckling on loins, leg or ribs; there was no tender choices to be held as a prize against the lips as the teeth ripped into cooked flesh, the face embracing all manner of delight; for all was bland here; and even though majestic feelings of grandeur enveloped them, for every morsel helped fill their guts, it all amounted to the same... food to get them from one day to the next.

Scurvy had remained a constant fear within the group in particular with the past death suffered amongst them, but little could be done other than for each, as an individual, to rip up the roots of any plant life that looked promising, to be devoured on the spot. Such morsels were never shared, always sheltered from prying eyes as they were devoured. Sharing was one thing, even with willem, but to leave oneself open to scurvy was not in the least looked upon as a nice way to die.

So greed had made its ugly presence early on in the days that followed after the shipwreck saw to their fate, but had quickly disappeared; and now, after many weeks, it had arrived again after a short absence. Some of the shipwrecked could feel the greed growing within them and others took what they found without giving it a second thought, yet some, like Pieter and Wiebbe, were quick to offer what they had to others, in particular Willem and Marinus.

Marinus was well on the mend and although he never complained about the pain in his arm and chest it was obviously present. Each time the man stood up, sat down, or moved abruptly, he could be heard to wince or be seen screwing up his face as his eyes closed tight. He was unable to throw a spear with full effect and even walking sometimes became a chore, the swinging motion of his arm taxing him over time and distance, though he never strayed too far from the camp fire.

Nevertheless, with the few unfortunate signs of greed and individuality came signs of comradeship and sharing, many conversations being carried into the night, accompanied by the howling of dingoes in the distance. They had learnt to stay away from unfavourable subjects such as women and wives, relying more on the questions which plagued them from day to day, where the different aspects of survival could be gnawed upon until an answer was derived. But it was all more of the same whereby the answers were not altogether reliable. Willem had once suggested that they make shoes from the bark of a tree. The basic shape could be cut from a tree and the bark strapped to the foot by rope or cordage, but the rope underfoot was unwieldy, the bark work crack and fall apart, there was too little choice when it came to variety in regards to durability, and the list went on.

But what more was there to do? Survival was their ultimate destiny and so on the morning of the eighteenth day of July the site which had been their home for over forty days was abandoned once and for all.

Everything that could help them in the survival and quest was taken along with them. They would head to the north where it

144

was known that ships from home would undeniably pass at one time or another, they in constant search of a better place in which to call their home; somewhere with a waterfall for bathing; some place thriving with meat and plenty of wood for which to corral their captives. They would do all they could to survive this land but the main boost to their decision in travelling north was to gain access to the native culture and their basic way of life, to fall upon their ways and techniques in gathering food and water. If a savage could inherit this land then there was no reason why an educated European could not do the same – but it was a shame that nature never bestowed favouritism to anyone other than those willing to adapt to the land itself and not vice versa.

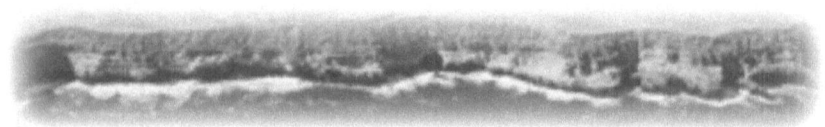

CHAPTER THIRTY-THREE

Willem and Pieter stood in front of the tree at the third campsite and tied into place the arrow they had made. It consisted of a shaft with two shorter pieces of wood attached to one end and made to resemble a pointer.

"Do you think it will work, Pieter?" asked Willem.

"I don't know, Willem," said he in return. "In all honesty I don't think we'll ever see them again, but if Cornelis and Joannes do come back this way they're sure to check each of the campsites for materials they might be able to use. At least if they see this they'll know which way to go in order to find us, but we'd be stupid beyond all contemplation to go south."

Pieter helped with the final knot and the two moved back to the second campsite to find everyone ready to go, not a single thing left behind that would be of use to them in their forage for food, forage for survival.

Each and every one of them carried his own blanket or sail cloth; every second man had a container of some description for porting water, whether big or small, and the others carried one of the three knives or makeshift spears.

They stood around the burnt out fire, a slight glow coming from some of the hotter embers deep within the mound of charcoal.

"We should have made a note for Cornelis and Joannes from the charcoal," said Marinus thinking how terrible it would be to be lost in a world yet undiscovered and moulded by the hand of man.

"The arrow that Willem made is a good enough sign," said Pieter as he looked from Marinus to the boy. "If they come this way again then they will see it."

"I just wish we could have done more for them," continued Marinus as he reflected further on the realities of their predicament. "Maybe we should wait a little longer; just a few more days."

"No," said Ariaen. "Our decision is made and we need to stand by it. Nothing is going to come easy. There'll be many upsets that will confront us. We have to remain loyal to ourselves first. We can't keep holding onto false hope."

"You're right," agreed Marinus. "Let's go; let's get out of here."

The group commenced their journey, their eyes falling upon their home for the final time, a seemingly sad farewell to a place they had come to know and trust, and now they were leaving it behind to search for something more rewarding.

Ariaen led the way north followed shortly after by Pieter and Willem.

"Come on, Marinus," urged Wiebbe, "time to go."

Marinus tagged onto the line followed closely by Seebaer and Jan, who between them carried several poles for erecting a shelter should the need arise when they stopped each night, a temporary solution to aid in protection should it rain, until such a time that something more permanent could be found. Much rope was also taken along.

Wiebbe took up the rear of the single file, glancing one final time over the site which had many memories, most of which he'd look forward to forgetting, but nevertheless, he said his goodbye to the site which had seen them mature from victims of a shipwreck to men of the world, and there was still plenty of room for growing.

CHAPTER THIRTY-FOUR

The group hadn't been gone long, less than five minutes in fact, when Marinus stopped in his tracks.

"What is it, Marinus?" asked Seebaer.

The others to his front also stopped and looked back to see what the matter was.

Marinus announced to everyone so that there was no mistake about what he was about to do, "I have to go back. We left no water."

"There's enough water in the rock hole," voiced Pieter from the front.

"No," said Marinus. That's almost gone," he looked to the ground and made his final decision. "I'm going back to leave my water at the third campsite. It'll make it easier to see the arrow."

"Marinus;" said Ariaen, "the animals will get at it."

"I'll hang it from a tree," insisted Marinus.

"You're wasting your time," said Jan, "and ours; and how are you to lift it with your arm like it is?"

Marinus was silent for a second before making a firm and final decision, "Don't wait for me," he said. "I'll catch up; I'll manage. All I have to do is follow the cliff; right?"

"That's right," said Wiebbe.

"Good; then you all go and I'll catch up soon."

"Are you sure?" asked Pieter.

"Yes; very sure."

"Take someone with you," suggested Pieter.

"I'll go," volunteered Willem.

"No," said Pieter. "You don't have the energy."

"No," assured Marinus. "I'll go alone; please. I need to do this for our friends."

A silent nod was all that was needed and Marinus headed off back towards the campsite to hang his water from the tree. He felt that it was the least he could do.

CHAPTER THIRTY-FIVE

Marinus stepped out upon the worn track which led up to the second campsite, and he was happy that he'd found his way so easily and without having to move nearer the cliff.

The slight pain he felt in his arm and chest was shrugged off as nothing more than a hindrance, as was his usual ploy. He turned to head towards the third campsite where just the day before they'd deposited the remains of some shellfish they'd managed to scrounge from the shoreline platform a little to the south. As he stepped out onto the nakedness of the site he was confronted by sheer surprise, four sets of gnarled teeth, viciousness he'd never seen or encountered before.

A deep throaty growl then surfaced from the first of the terrors which looked deep within his eye and then a second, and a third, then a fourth. Two of them commenced to encircle him, preventing him from escape, feeling within them that he was alone and susceptible to their whims.

Dingoes; massive and hungry for easy prey. They could sense the inabilities of Marinus, sense his fear; could smell the water that he carried, and above all his weakness. It wasn't their normal practise to attack something so large but they'd been known to take down large kangaroos and aboriginal women too frail to protect themselves, women left against their will to fend for themselves by a tribe unwilling to feed them in old age.

There was no sport in catching prey; it was simply a matter of survival, to take what you could get and when you could get it. Marinus was simply an easy target, frail, wounded, doused in fear, and a good source of meat and water.

The animals closed in upon him and then the attack came, from the rear, his calf bitten into.

CHAPTER THIRTY-SIX

The cry that filled the air was heinous to say the least, the worst death cry that the men had heard their entire lives. All they could do was stop, turn and stare, looking out in the direction from whence the cries came. And it soon fell silent.

"We should go back," urged Willem, "and help our friend."

"No!" said Jan. "It was his own foolish decision."

"It wasn't foolish to want to help a friend, no more foolish than it is for Willem to want to provide help to Marinus," said Ariaen.

"But it's too late now. Marinus has met with a power greater than his own." said Jan.

"Those damn savages," spat Seebaer. "No good can come of them. They'll kill us all."

"He's right," said Seebaer. "The savages of this land can't be relied upon. We can't befriend them. They're uncharitable. They're swine; damn swines, each and every one of them."

"You see," said Jan. "They're cannibals, every last one of them."

"He's right," said Pieter. "Why kill Marinus for no good reason?"

"Maybe it wasn't the natives," advised Wiebbe. "Maybe it was a snake or something else."

"One of those dogs," suggested Ariaen.

"No. No, no, no; you're wrong," insisted Seebaer. "That's no dog that made him scream like that; no snake either. The savages were waiting for us to leave, watching our every move. They see us, they know where we are. We've seen them before, haven't we: some of us, have we not?"

"Yes, that's true," said Jan. "They've had plenty of time to show themselves. Why haven't they?"

"Maybe they're scared of us," said Ariaen.

"No; they're not scared. They've had plenty of time. No savage would wait as long as this before coming forward if his intentions were honourable."

"Then what do you suggest?" asked Ariaen of Seebaer and the others as he looked around, and the men moved into a tight ball during the preceding minute, to more easily access the situation and talk of war.

"Kill them," said Jan.

"Don't be stupid," spat Wiebbe. "We're too few."

"There is only one solution," insisted Ariaen. "We must continue north and hope for rescue."

"And if rescue doesn't come?" asked Seebaer.

"Then we find somewhere that will sustain us; find some savages that won't kill us," came the call for calm from Ariaen.

"I don't trust these people," said Seebaer. "I think it's time we had a new leader, someone more readily able to see to our needs."

Ariaen remained calm on hearing those words as did Pieter who stood beside him. Each and every one of them thought upon the call for an immediate election, the call for a change in leadership.

"Listen to me," said Ariaen, unforgiving, knowing the others around him better than he'd ever let be known. "If you wish for new leadership then you go off by yourself and find it. Pieter, Willem and Wiebbe are coming with me. What do you say, Jan? Are you with me or Seebaer?"

Jan could see the manipulation of the talk, as could Seebaer.

"Stop," said Seebaer holding up his palms in defeat, a funny little smirk upon his face. "I see where this is leading; do you take me for a fool? I'll stay with you, Ariaen. I'll not cause any further trouble, but remember this: we all have the right to voice our own opinions."

"So long as it's an opinion and not a confrontation for mutiny or war, then you are free to voice all you want. We need to survive... I suggest we continue on our way and do just that."

CHAPTER THIRTY-SEVEN

20th July.

The sun broke the horizon when an aboriginal fell upon the scene of Marinus ripped to shreds. All of the signs were there; it was a pack of dingoes.

He gazed around with his spear in hand and looked upon the tree, seeing an arrow made from wood, a curious device, its reason for being completely eluding him. And then it hit him hard. The white spirits had left a message that they were heading through the Malgana territory and towards the Yinggarda people. That's why the spirits - these people - had failed to make contact with them, they belonged elsewhere. But what of the other two spirits that had been found so recently?

Barega was his name, an aboriginal of the Malgana people, of the Wayle tribe. He was a tall fellow of handsome features, deep creases within his face displaying great character. He stood naked with a small shield and a spear, a small cloak of fur carried around his shoulder, a gift from the Nanda to the south, the people of that vicinity who had an interest in a marital corroboree in the near future.

Barega felt the urge bite into him, his new call to duty. He would have to provide this news to his elders for it was all of great interest. Many of his tribe and others around had heard of the white spirits that had fallen upon their land, making visit upon them from across the ocean. It was all new to him and very bewildering. Many times in the past were ships seen passing them by, out to sea and at full sail, and never in all that time did Barega or his people know anything about the strange site; but now they knew. The ships carried the spirits of the dead.

The Wayle tribe were currently camped several days walk away, after calculating stops for food and water. There was certainly no rush and Barega had all the time in the world but news on the spirits would have to be passed as soon as possible. If their intention was indeed to lay a visit upon those of the Yinggarda then the Malgana would have to make sure the way for them was kept clear. And then something more troubled him. How was it that a spirit of the dead could be killed by a pack of dingoes? If these visitors were indeed ancestors of the living then surely they'd not be able to perish as they would have once done at a time when they walked the earth.

Barega saw the obvious. Blood was everywhere, flesh and tendons bare to the world of the living.

This wasn't the spirit of the dead; how could it be?

CHAPTER THIRTY-EIGHT

The group of survivors continued reluctantly on their way to the north, pressing on into the misery that encased them.

It had become curiously clear that the natives of the land sought nothing more than to segregate them and have them killed one by one, a systematic elimination of the trespassers upon their land. Seebaer felt he could see more clearly than the others, that the cannibals were keeping them alive on purpose, and short of providing them with food and water, were treating them no different than they would cattle.

Seebaer could not restrain himself any longer, the episode of death two days before playing too much on his mind, "Stop; wait," said he from the rear.

"We need to keep walking," pressed Wiebbe.

"Stop, I say," repeated Seebaer. "Listen to me, all of you. Don't you see," he continued as the others gathered around. "They're killing us off, one by one; eating us at their leisure."

"That's ridiculous," urged Pieter. "Why would they do that?"

"Why would they walk naked in the glistering heat and freezing cold?" replied Seebaer. "I don't know their ways but it's clear to me now that they're intention is to eat us, one and all," he turned to Jan. "You heard Marinus scream; did you not?"

"Aye," said Jan, "The most terrible scream I've ever heard."

"Seebaer, you're ridiculous," said Wiebbe. "But presume you're correct about them, what would you have us do?"

"We must fight," he said, "stand and deliver... all that and more."

"Seebaer," said Pieter calmly. "We have rope, a shelter, blankets, a little water and three knives with a couple of makeshift spears. We are hungry, without the energy to work hard like men and have a boy... a young man to look after. How are we supposed to wage war against an enemy that is far stronger than we are, carry weapons which they are obviously experienced at using, and know the land like the back of their hand?"

"I don't know, but we must think of something."

"We're going to head north, Seebaer; all of us; I'm tired of repeating myself," said Ariaen. "There is safety in numbers. Stay if you wish. I still think you're wrong. I have no explanation for Marinus and don't intend to waste my time searching for one. Return to the old camp and you could end up like him. If you honestly believe that he was eaten by the natives then stay here and wait for them to come for you. As for me and the others, we continue north."

Seebaer was silent for a moment but quickly came to his senses, realising that his petty feud was useless, that Wiebbe, Pieter and Willem would not do anything to disrupt the friendship between them and Ariaen.

"Okay, I'll take my orders like a good soldier does," said Seebaer sarcastically.

"No one's pressing you to take orders, Seebaer, and no orders are being given. Decision rests with the best answer and the majority," said Ariaen, hoping to settle the argument by pointing out the obvious.

So they continued on their way with little further said until only a few short hours later, just before noon, when they came across what appeared to be a deep well dug into the ground, a poorly constructed hole in which to catch water.

The group fell upon it with excitement and quickly tied their empty water containers to pieces of rope, lowering each into the seemingly shallow well in order to get water from it; and they weren't disappointed.

It wasn't long before they were all full with water and sat in their exhausted state in a small semi-circle around the well, looking upon it with admiration even though it was not built of stone and cement.

"Where do you suppose this came from?" asked Wiebbe of Seebaer.

"You're trying to tell me that the natives aren't savages, that they possess ideas and abilities," said Seebaer.

"It's all there, right in front of you," said Wiebbe. "Take from it what you will. Any person able to live off a desert land like this one deserves more praise than can be afforded. Look around you, Seebaer. This place is of the devil's own making. To survive here you need guts and determination."

Seebaer stood up then, "I have to go for a walk... to relieve myself of this pain in my gut. Are you coming, Jan."

"Will Jan help the pain?" asked Wiebbe.

"He'll keep me company whilst I have my pants down around my ankles."

And without further ado the two walked off towards where the cliff lay in order to take time from the group and do as they needed to do.

Ariaen waited for the two men to disappear from view and were out of earshot, "Let them be," he said, "Don't encourage argument, please."

"I'm not like you, Ariaen," said Wiebbe. "I can't put up with the pessimism like you. You handle yourself very well and in all situations. I wish I was more like you. But I must say this, I—."

"Look," interrupted Wiebbe, "don't be startled; listen carefully. There... see."

The group of four looked up and saw six aboriginal men not more than eighty feet away.

They wore little adornment apart from four of them wearing what appeared to be small cloaks used to keep the cold at bay, blankets of fur from animals which the survivors didn't know were employed as blankets by night. Each of them also wore a waist belt and arm bands. Three of the men carried several small lizards which hung from their belts, kills that had been secured by the weapons they carried, which were numerous and diverse, including several spears and different types of boomerangs, bent sticks of which the survivors had never seen before. One of them carried a hatchet, a thick stick with a stone head attached quite securely with human hair made into rope.

The natives looked at each other and it was clear that one of them was talking to the others, their eyes fixed upon the survivors. Several nods of the head were then seen and one of the six stepped forward, followed shortly by the others. Once the distance between the two had been halved they stopped, the survivors having stood.

"Show no fear," said Adriane. "Smile and be friendly."

"Are these the spirits?" asked Kulan.

"I think so," answered Narrah. "But maybe they're men, like the others."

"What did they say?" asked Pieter, his question going unanswered, a simple 'shush' being emitted from Wiebbe.

The six natives fell silent and looked again upon the strange men until Kulan stepped forward, away from the others at his side and made his approach in peace, taking a small goanna from his belt in his right hand and offering it to them.

"Take this food; it's good," said Kulan. "The yellow fat of the goanna is a delicacy amongst my people."

"He's offering you something," said Pieter of the obvious. "Quickly, take it or we'll be offending them."

Wiebbe took the food and smiled, bowing slightly, "Thank you."

Kulan stepped back and turned to the others, smiling, "You see; they're happy to receive it, just like the other two. They must know what it is."

"They look at it in such a strange way," said Nioka. "Show him that you killed it, that's it's a gift for him and his people."

It was unknown to the survivors that dance was a formality of communication in many ways. This was a corroboree and involved movement, often imitating animals and actions, hunters or bouts of conflict. All such movements told a story and many new ones were developed as new stories arose to be told, to be recorded for all time, the very history of the tribe being passed from one generation to the next. Most were accompanied by music but in respect of the current situation it was done without.

Kulan crouched low, knees bent and buttocks almost touching the ground, his spear taken a good grip of and poised in a throwing stance. Kulan moved around and then stood there silently before the men, a grimace of anger portrayed upon his face, the spear leveraged in Wiebbe's direction as though ready to kill him.

A knife suddenly appeared out of the blue, flying through the air with great precision and penetrating deep into the stomach of Kulan. The look upon the native's face was one of great shock and bewilderment as he looked up and saw Seebaer standing there behind the other four.

Narrah and the other natives, Nioka, Pindara, Daku and Woorin acted promptly and readied their spears as they pressed in on the survivors, voicing their anger at the suddenness of the attack, an unprovoked and unnecessary act of betrayal.

"No! Stop!" yelled Cornelis as he and Joannes came running up from the rear followed by another two aboriginals, Barwon and Kalti.

The stirred emotions of the other five were abated slightly but vengeance had filled their minds.

Ariaen, Wiebbe and Pieter could not believe their eyes, nor could Willem, the murder of the native, for no good reason, being delivered without second thought, Seebaer endangering their lives as though they meant nothing to him.

It was clear, all of it, that the men who had shipped from South Africa were about to meet their end unless reprisal was performed. The presence of Cornelis and Joannes had proved beyond any doubt that the natives were friendly. They had given food and shown friendship. To now be struck down for the whims of a single man was simply senseless.

What was to become of them now?

Ariaen pulled the knife that he carried from his waist belt and within the blink of an eye rushed over to Seebaer and penetrated the point of his blade deep into him. The facial grimace of Seebaer was different from that of Kulan's; Seebaer's grimace was of horror and pain.

The commotion all around was full of emotion. The aboriginals had congregated around their fallen friend, looking up periodically at Ariaen and the dead Seebaer. And then Jan came to view, having crouched behind some bush to escape the horrors of being eaten alive. He had believed Seebaer to the fullest, understood what it was he'd been saying about these horrible natives. But he was wrong.

Cornelis and Joannes did well over the following minutes, comforting their new friends and showing they cared for the dead by embracing Kulan's fallen body, him being dead and void of life. It was this alone that settled the calamity of the situation, bringing the anger to a simmer, the simmer to a calm.

Wiebbe had pulled the bloodied knife from Seebaer as he fell dead and holding the blade had moved very slowly over to Narrah. He held the knife out and offered it to him.

"No!" yelled Jan from the rear. "What are you doing? Are you mad? You're insane; stupid beyond all comprehension." He turned and started to run, running towards the cliffs of the coast and on reaching the edge leaped into the air and fell to his death upon the shoreline platform below, secure in his own mind that he had escaped being eaten alive, that the pain of death he had delivered unto himself was far less than what would have been delivered by the savages he saw before him. But it was his mind that was corrupted, and only his. He failed to see what the others had seen, and had believed all that he had been told by Seebaer. Seebaer was his death, Seebaer and his own infliction, an affliction of the mind that could not be removed.

CHAPTER THIRTY-NINE

The afternoon had finally arrived, the sun seeking the horizon, and as the fire blazed in all its glory the men sat around it, not in their groups of white and black, but seated in equal terms, one survivor between two natives and one native between two whites: where possible.

There was plenty of food being cooked upon the fire as flames appeared here and there, and there was water in abundance. The aboriginals were pleasant and friendly, and seemingly content with the actions of Wiebbe, for he had inflicted justice upon one of his own in the face of the controversy, in similar fashion to how they saw justice delivered, but they usually maimed, rarely killed. Seebaer had done wrong by the Wayle and justice had been delivered.

"I still can't believe that you're alive," said Ariaen to Cornelis.

"Yes," Cornelis agreed, "hard to believe that we fell in with such good fortune. We've had plenty to eat since we were found by Barwon and Kalti," two aboriginal men looked to Cornelis when their names were mentioned.

"You know them by name, that's impressive," said Pieter.

"We've learnt quite a bit already. We haven't seen their main camp yet but I believe it won't be long now."

"How do you know?" asked Wiebbe.

"Do you see any women sitting around the fire?" asked Cornelis.

"What are they talking about?" asked Barwon.

"I don't know," said Kalti. He looked into Cornelis' eyes. "What are you talking about, Cornelis?"

"What did he say?" asked Wiebbe.

"It's beyond me," answered Cornelis. "He heard his name called."

"Ask him about the women," prodded Wiebbe.

"Where are the women," asked Cornelis and shaped the cup of a woman's breasts with his hands held at his chest."

"Ahhh," said Barwon, "He wants a woman."

"Then that confirms it all," said Kalti. "They're not spirits. Maybe we should get them a woman, each and every one of them."

"Including the small one?" asked Barwon, talking of Willem.

"Especially him," answered Kalti. "The time for marriage is near. We'll pass the word onto the Yinggarda as the agreement with the Nanda has already been struck."

"Maybe the Yinggarda won't want them," said Narrah. "Look at them. They look sick. We'll see what the Nanda can do for us."

"They're different," insisted Barwon. "Maybe we can learn from them. A man that can float on water in a craft so big and large must know something."

"Well," said Nioka. "They come from somewhere, a place that can't be seen."

"Are you sure they're not spirits?" asked Woorin. "They scare me."

"The elders will tell us, but meanwhile we must make the best of the situation and return when the sun rises once more."

Barwon looked into Cornelis' eyes, "Not far now and we can talk of women, when the sun crosses the sky and we have walked towards that direction," he said, indicating the north-east with his lips after making an arch through the air with his arm, "then we shall be home."

"One day away," said Cornelis, "I think."

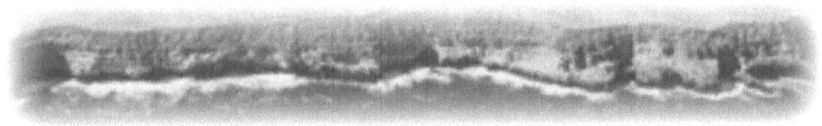

CHAPTER FORTY

21st July.

They slept soundly that night and awoke the following morning to be provided more food, the natives sitting around the fire and talking of the day's journey, and after an hour of relaxed contemplation and feeding the group was hurried to be ready to move, ushered by their new found friends to stand.

Wiebbe and Pieter moved over to the poles and cloth that they used as a shelter but the natives shook their heads and tried with great effort to convey that the objects would only weigh them down.

"Leave it all here," said Joannes. "Bring the knives and the water containers, nothing more. We won't need them."

"You're right," said Ariaen. "We need to learn new ways of living."

Cornelis looked at Ariaen as he was pulling his hand away and saw in his eye that there was something he found hard to come to grips with; an abstract of his old life. "Do you have any tobacco left?" he asked, prodding a response.

"No," answered Ariaen. "We smoked the last, remember."

"I was hoping, that's all."

"Here," said Ariaen and pulled the empty tobacco box from his pocket, "see for yourself."

"I trust you," said Cornelis.

Ariaen simply smiled and threw the empty box into the fire, looking at it as it landed in the coals, where it would remain undisturbed for more than two hundred and seventy years, before being found by a white man in the future. He looked up then and saw that the last of the natives had almost disappeared from view.

"Come old friend," said Ariaen. "It's time to go. I don't wish to be lost."

"I don't think there's much chance of that happening," said Cornelis. You'd soon be found again," and Ariaen knew that he was referring to the tracking abilities of the natives they had befriended.

CHAPTER FORTY-ONE

The survivors had taken their first real step in cohabitation with the natives, the aboriginals of the land, and as time passed they commenced to learn of many new things.

Aboriginals lived together in tribes, made up exclusively of family members who formed a clan, each clan being responsible for ensuring the well-being of the land on which they dwelled. They lived with the land, not the land with them.

Tribes had many rules, many regulations, and this included the segregation of men and women into separate roles, tasks also divided according to age. Men hunted with spears and fished. They hunted animals such as kangaroos, wallabies, echidnas and possums, reptiles and birds. They used spears and boomerangs to hit, catch and kill, and could scale trees in order to get their food.

They hunted in groups and sometimes as individuals, and where there was an abundance of bellies to be filled the catch was shared equally amongst all. Boys coming of age often went with their father to learn how to hunt, to make and use tools and weapons. All children earned their place in their society. Values such as respecting elders and other social responsibilities were of great importance and older children also cared for the elderly too frail to tend themselves.

Women were also very important in the day-to-day survival of the clan, gathering the bulk of the food which was eaten on a daily basis, and they were also responsible for gathering medicine. Girls almost always went with their mothers to learn about bush food and bush medicine. Education of the younger children also came under the sway of the women and older siblings. Women also decided when girls would undergo rituals in preparation for marriage, they acted as midwives and story-tellers.

Each tribe had an Elder. He decided when to move camp and settled disputes. Elders were those considered to be wise in tribal knowledge and worldly matters. They decided when boys would be initiated and when girls would be married after having received their ritual.

It was all such an intricate network of rules and standards, but overall their way of life was rather simple and unhurried, very relaxing and maintained a pleasant mood for all as they abided by the laws laid down. It was now simply a time for the survivors of the Zuytdorp to not just interact with the natives but to become a part of them.

But of all the most important attributes that the aboriginals had in play, the most important was the medicine man.

He was a powerful man, and was responsible for curing many physical ills, sometimes by massage and sometimes by sucking, removing the evil that caused the pain; sometimes he would administer natural medicines made from plants or roots. The emphasis on healing was on the spirit, not the body. Their belief that the spirit was the source of their illness empowered the medicine man to treat the sick. Sometimes however an individual was struck down by evil magic of another medicine man or powerful omen. The victim would usually become sick and die, not necessarily because the magic had worked well, but because the individual believed in the magic.

There were also Corroborees, each of which was of great importance to a tribe, it was their living history. There were two types of corroboree; the secretive, held during initiation ceremonies, and secular, which was a majority of what was held in full view of the survivors. The secretive was a gift to be awarded to an individual during his changing years from youth to adulthood, a change which saw many varieties of custom being performed and enacted.

It was common for a ceremony to be opened after five minutes of music and chants from instruments and throats. Beating a waddy against a shield, growing shouts, howling and didgeridoos; singers and dancers would join in, enacting a piece of historical past and of secular importance, and on special occasion these could go on for many hours, people having painted their bodies with natural earth pigments red and yellow ochres, white clay, and black charcoal. Bird down, plant down, flowers and seeds, many hues and shapes were employed during different ceremonies.

Once again, made clear to some, but not all, the survivors came to accept that they were being adopted. First the tribe would accept them and then the land would accept them. This was the accepted way of life. It was systematic. Tribal acceptance came before survival could be taught. There were many secrets that the land possessed and the aboriginals knew a vast majority of them, in particular the area in which they lived. Hunter-gatherers they were, and much ground was to be covered by the survivors in the years to fall before them, and with those years a vast knowledge of understanding would become so clear that it was as though standing in front of them all of the time. One thing of great importance was water and many wells, soaks, and rock holes existed upon the land, but only a few of the tribe knew them all. Along with their water sources came sacred ground, ground on which only a designated few were permitted to enter, one or two individuals of an entire tribe permitted access during specific rituals and ceremonies.

The survivors of the Zuytdorp had a lot to learn and at the present they were little more than observers. But as time passed more and more became clear to them all.

They hadn't yet been accepted to be a part of a 'sacred' corroboree but almost all other aspects of tribal life were showered upon them.

They were near the beginning of a new life and the only aspect of their survival was the barrier created by their language and of their morbid lives as single men. Each had a growing desire for a woman and Willem was also coming of age.

CHAPTER FORTY-TWO

21st November, 1712.

It had been four months since they'd come into contact with the Wayle tribe and the relationship was good; very good.

The campsite in which they now called home was split into family groups where each maintained its own fire. They came together during the evenings and made visits upon one another to prepare for a hunt or other activity which included excursions for the women into the vastness surrounding them to look for an assortment of food, be it seed, fruit, berries or small insects for making up what the hunters failed to kill.

It was now mid-afternoon and Ariaen approached the other five members of his 'clan', sitting down amongst them as Willem stoked the fire, Pieter and Cornelis shaped their spear points, and Joannes prepared for cooking: ever since the episode with the knife, where Kulan was killed by Seebaer, the instruments of death were cast aside as something evil. Such a valuable tool and it was discarded within the blink of an eye.

"Where's Wiebbe?" asked Ariaen.

"He was invited out for a short hunt by Pindara."

"Good," said Ariaen. "I have some news," and he smiled in Willem's direction.

"What is it?" he asked. "What are you looking at me like that for?"

"Firstly let me say that I've just been communicating with a man named Barega. I'm sure the tribe has been trying to tell us this for some time now but the point never got across. It appears that Marinus was killed by a dingo."

"I knew there was a perfect explanation," said Pieter.

"So why are you smiling?" asked Willem.

"Barega was organising a marital corroboree with the people to the south, the Nanda. It's a few days walk and all of the Malgana will attend."

"And..." insisted Willem.

"You're to be wedded, Willem, married off," smiled Ariaen.

"Married? But I'm not ready... not well," he pleaded.

"You're young, Willem," pointed out Ariaen. "It's the best thing for you; really. You have a long life to live and there's only one way to live a life on this land."

"But we might still be rescued," said Willem with a little confidence.

"Do you know what I believe, Willem?" said Pieter as he looked at the boy, a concerned look of worry caking his face. "Once you've spent several years here with these people you won't want to return home."

"Don't talk nonsense," said Joannes. "I wouldn't care if I was married to ten wives; I'd be the first one aboard if I saw a ship sail past."

"You'd have to live on the coast in order to see a ship, Joannes, and the coast doesn't provide all the necessities of life for the Malgana."

"But married," said Willem again. "Whose idea was it?"

"It must have been one of the elders, and if I had to make a guess I would assume Woorak. It's so hard to understand these people sometimes. Do you know, I was asking Daku how far it was to the marital corroboree and he said it was not far. 'No long,' he said, 'little, short,' and then he indicated to me that it would take twelve or fourteen days to get there."

"Yes, well... I'm picking up a little of the language but I'm finding it very hard," said Cornelis.

"Yes, you are," said Ariaen as he erupted in another smile.

"I don't like the look on your face either," said Cornelis.

"You are rather young, too," replied Ariaen.

"No, you can't," Cornelis stood up. "Not married, not to the Nanda. I don't mind the women, it's not that at all, but I'd prefer for us to stay together."

"Willem will wed and his wife will reside here, I'm sure that's the intention. And as for you, young friend, one of the young women right here has taken a fancy to you," said Ariaen.

"Not Kyeema, surely," said Cornelis.

"Afraid so," said Ariaen. "The women folk have seen you two at play. You should be more careful. Your manhood has revealed much to the women of this camp."

"And who here isn't man enough to have needs?" stated Cornelis. "I'm not the only one that's been corrupted by my needs as a man."

"I'm sure you're right," said Ariaen, "but if it comes from the elders then I don't think you're going to have much choice. It seems the decision has been made for you."

"How many days did you say till—?"

"Twelve to fourteen," interrupted Pieter.

"And we depart tomorrow," finished Ariaen.

CHAPTER FORTY-THREE

The campsite had been packed and everyone was ready to move, only the essentials going with them.

This was the first time the survivors had moved camp with the natives and it was interesting to note that the camp itself was left intact with the grinding stones left upon the ground where they were used. Shelters were left as they were the night before, sheets of bark propped up with branches and the fire was simply smothered with sand and the hotter pieces of half burnt wood carried in other wooden containers to aid in starting the next camp fire when it came time to setting up a temporary site.

A small group of men lead the way; Narrah, Pindara, Kalti and Barega. Hunter-gatherers they were, always on the lookout for food, never turning down an opportunity to secure a meal for the tribe and as the day wore on the group found itself some distance from the others but would rejoin them later.

The days were long and hard for the survivors, still suffering from acclimatisation, their bodies still getting used to their surroundings. There was a noted difference between the two: the natives and the Europeans. The natives were largely thin and tall, with slender legs from the constant walking; they on the other hand were not built for long treks over rough terrain where the soles of their feet bore the brunt of the heat and vegetation. It would take an eternity to get one's feet used to the conditions.

They were travelling in a direction away from the setting sun and the further they went the more eastward they seemed to go. It wasn't for the survivors to question the direction, for the motive was well known, but the path they took seemed weirdly peculiar rather than straight forward.

After eleven day of walking they came upon a rock in the distance and Daku came up to Ariaen. The aboriginal pursed his lips and pointed with his mouth towards the object of rock silhouette against the clear skyline.

"Walga," said Daku, "Walga, Walga."

"What's that all about?" asked Wiebbe as they continued walking.

"I'm presuming that the rock formation up ahead is called Walga," announced Ariaen.

"Walga," said Daku again, confirming Ariaen's suspicions.

"That must be the ceremonial grounds," said Pieter.

"Maybe," agreed Ariaen, and then, "maybe not," and continued with the walk.

It didn't take long after that for all to realise that they were near the end of their long trek and some were growing anxious in regards to the ceremony that was to take place, but not Kyeema who smiled when she looked at Cornelis, and he too smiled back though deep down felt as though he should wait awhile before surrendering himself to a culture he wasn't sure was for him; but what choice did he have? His very survival depended upon it and he loved the idea of having children, regardless of the colour of their skin.

When they finally came upon the foot of the rock formation the women set about putting a camp together whilst some of the men took to a place where they knew an opening existed within the rock.

It didn't take long for the survivors to be introduced to the mouth of the cave and soon after several bark plates with a variety of colours were brought forth.

Ariaen and the others watched with great attentiveness as Woorin and Daku commenced to draw upon the wall of the cave entrance and what they drew shocked them to the very core.

These two men who had led them here were painting a picture, a piece of art, using charcoal and red ochre mixed with water along with other colours derived from plants that the women had gathered. It was a mural of sorts in dedication to these strange men from across the sea. They had been accepted by the Nanda and were now a part of their history. Right before them a sailing ship was being painted.

A tear welled in Ariaen's eyes and Willem asked him a question, "What are you crying for?"

"Because we have found our way, young Willem. We are now at peace with the land and with the people, never to return to Europe. We have a future here now. This is now our home."

Ariaen smiled at Woorin and Daku, they in turn smiled back, on this the happiest day of Ariaen's life.

Their history had now been recorded and they would never be forgotten. But this wasn't the end of their journey, for the corroboree was not very far away, and within time all of the survivors, all of them, were married in one of the most magnificent ceremonies the aboriginals had to offer.

www.ingramcontent.com/pod-product-compliance
Lightning Source LLC
Chambersburg PA
CBHW030636120726
47904CB00006B/2177